Matt

Black Tuxedos MC Book Three

Darlene Tallman

Contents

MATT

The Black Tuxedos MC

INTERNATIONAL BESTSELLING AUTHOR
DARLENE TALLMAN

Copyright

This is a work of fiction. Names, characters, places, and incidents are either the product of the author's imagination or used fictitiously, and any resemblance to actual persons, living or dead, business establishments, events or locales is entirely coincidental.

Editors: Mary Kern, Shannon McFadden, Nicole McVey, Jeni Clancy, Beth DiLoreto, Melanie Gray
Formatter: Liberty Parker
Cover by Tracie Douglas of Dark Water Covers

Dedication

For Mandie, who wanted Matt from the first time she read "Reese". I hope you enjoy your fictional man!

Acknowledgments

These are always hard because I'm worried about forgetting folks! Suffice it to say, I have to acknowledge my two PAs, Nicole Lloyd and Sharon Renee, who do their best to keep me organized and on some semblance of a path. My girls, who read and offer suggestions along the way - Jeni, Shannon, Beth, Nicole, Melanie, Mary - couldn't do this without y'all, not even gonna try. Liberty - who proofs behind me and also offers suggestions when I get "stuck". My cover designer, Tracie, who always comes through with the best cover for me. And last but not least, the readers, who have been chomping at the bit for Matt's story.

Blurb

When Matt Ferguson got severely injured during his last deployment, he thought he'd come home and marry his high school sweetheart and they'd live happily ever after. That dream crashed and burned when she left him after cruelly hurling words that still impact him to this day. Eventually, he finds a home with the Black Tuxedos MC and is now running the construction company that the MC owns. He's lonely, but he knows there's no woman alive who'll deal with the problem he has, so he resolves to do what he can, where he can, even though all he wants is someone who he can love and who will love him back.

Mandie Matchum was dealt a crappy hand, but as her foster mother always told her, you make the best of what you've got and she's trying. Raising two small children on her own with no support, she's struggling to finish up her degree while working as a waitress at a local restaurant. She's noticed the handsome biker but doesn't think he'd ever want someone like her and anyhow, she's no good at relationships so why bother?

Can two people who've lost faith in love still build a life together? Will they each overcome their past to forge a new future?

This book is rated for ages 18+ due to subject matter and adult themes

Black Tuxedos MC Members

Reese - President (Corrie)
Porter - VP (Kirsten)
Matt - VP's Enforcer (Mandie)
Motor - President's Enforcer
Nick – Patched Member (Shayla)
Specks - IT
Ripper - SAA
Atlas - Road Captain
Doughboy - Treasurer
Chrome – Secretary
Rex – Patched Member (Lacey)
Pug - Patched Member
Slim Jim - Patched Member
Jacob - Prospect

Joseph - Prospect
Garrison - Prospect

PROLOGUE

Matt

I DON'T LIKE THIS FEELING, AS IF OUR UNIT IS BEING *watched.* The hairs on the nape of my neck have been standing upright for the past thirty minutes, ever since we arrived at a small village. "Ferguson," my commanding officer barks out, his voice tense. "Take Gumby, Jackal, Coast, and Liner and check out that building to your left. The rest of us will investigate the one on the right."

"10-4," I reply. I motion with my hand and the men that I lead get in step behind me. Once we're huddled together, I advise, "We're checking on that building over there. Keep alert; my gut is saying something's not right." Each of them nods to show they understand, and we begin slowly inching our way across to the derelict building. We've been doing this for too long not to recognize that something is 'off' with this whole situation and each

1

of my men is as wired as I am. It's obvious that this area has seen its fair share of warfare, with the buildings all in disrepair and not a soul in sight.

We've made it to the building itself and are spreading out when I hear the unmistakable sound of an RPB being launched toward us. "Run!" Gumby screams. I'm halfway back to the 'road' when the blast detonates. I feel like the left side of my body is on fire as I fall to the ground and roll.

"We got you, Fergie," Jackal informs me. I don't know how much time has passed; everything is a fog and my brain is rattled enough, I can't even think of what just transpired. He repeats himself so I look up at him and see he's covered in blood – so much blood that it can't just be his, only I don't know whose it is and my head is pounding so badly that I can't form the words so I can ask.

As the pain radiates throughout my body, blissful dark-ness claims me.

I wake up in the hospital, the left side of my body covered in bandages. I know I'm in pain, but I suspect it's not nearly as bad as it could be. Right now, I'm by myself. I don't know how long I've been here and have no clue how the rest of the men in my unit fared, although I have a vague memory of Jackal pulling me to safety. Spying the hospital bed remote, I push the button that has what looks like a nurse's cap on it. When a tinny voice comes across, I manage to croak out, "I'm awake but need some help."

"We'll be right in, Sergeant," the voice responds. While I wait, I play with the remote and manage to move the bed into a better, more comfortable position.

A few minutes later, a corpsman comes in and moves to my side. "Can I get something to drink? My throat hurts," I rasp out.

"Let me get your vitals checked and I'll be glad to get that for you, Sergeant," the pretty little corpsman replies. She quickly and efficiently checks my pulse, takes my blood pressure, and presses a few buttons on the machine that I'm hooked to once she hangs two new bags of solution on the IV pole, after she checked my name and birthdate. Once she's done with that, she places a straw inside the giant plastic cup and holds it close so I can take a few sips. "Your throat is sore because up until last night, you were on a ventilator."

"Why?" I feel like I gargled with shards of glass and my voice sounds like it as well.

"You were in a medically-induced coma, Sergeant, so the worst of your injuries could heal."

"How long have I been here? Where are my men? What's wrong with me?" Questions swirl in my head and cohesive thoughts are impossible.

She evades my questions and says, "I'll let the doctor know you're awake." She maneuvers the table across me so that I can easily reach the cup, before she puts on gloves and takes care of the bag that's attached to the side of the bed. When she sees my look of concern, she states, "It's just a catheter. Once your doctor has checked you over, if he says we can, we'll remove it and you'll be able to take yourself to the bathroom. It won't be easy at first, but we'll get you back on your feet."

I nod, exhaustion taking root once again. I notice what looks like a pain pump and ask, "Is this for my pain meds?"

"Yes, you can self-administer them. The dosage is titrated so that you can't overdose yourself. Please, make sure that *if you're feeling pain that you use it; don't try to be a hero. Your body has endured a lot and needs to heal. Rest and managing your pain will help accomplish that."*

"Thank you, Doc," I state. I have no clue how badly I'm hurt or even how much time has lapsed, but she's been compassionate and kind.

"You're welcome. Now rest until the doctor gets here. Like I said, I'll let him know you're awake, but he's due to show up in the next hour or so and it's unlikely that you'll see him before then." I give her a thumbs up because it really does hurt to talk right now, then reach over and push the button on my pain pump. As the cool liquid hits my IV and I feel it coursing through my veins, I allow sleep to reclaim me.

I've been in the hospital for two weeks now, with the first four days completely a blank thanks to the medically induced coma. Today, I'm being discharged to a rehab facility so that I can hopefully recover some of the muscle and strength that I lost due to my injuries. As I stare in the mirror, I cringe at the damage I can see. My face and the front of my body are covered with bruises and abra-

sions where I hit the ground. It's my back, however, that has me concerned. Fucking RPG damn near killed me; in fact, I'm the only survivor from my unit, a fact that has me swimming in guilt. Jackal, the man who saved me and one of my closest friends, succumbed to his injuries. But he fought until the very end, something that I hope I'm able to do if the situation ever arises. Of course, it won't be as part of the U.S. military. Seems Uncle Sam doesn't want those of us who have been nearly blown to pieces.

Taking a deep breath, I grab the other mirror and turn so I can fully see how things are healing. Most of my injuries are contained to the left side of my body, starting at my shoulder area, wrapping down my left flank, across my ass and to the front of my left thigh. Thank God my junk didn't get hit. A random thought, I know, all things considered, but I think my fiancé, Jessa, will be happy about that fact. Granted, I haven't seen her yet; she's been 'busy' but is planning to visit me in rehab. I'm still unsure if I'll be showing her all of this quite yet. Guess it depends on whether or not she asks.

I'm one of the lucky ones, though. I needed some skin grafts, but for the most part, the areas will heal. I'll bear the scars, but it is what it is. I'm alive and that's the important thing.

"Are you ready to go, Sergeant?" the corpsman calls out. I quickly put my shirt on and leave the bathroom.

"Yeah. How long will I be in rehab?" I question, grabbing the duffle bag of things I've managed to accumulate. While Jessa wasn't able to see me, she did send me some clothes so I'm not leaving in a fucking hospital gown with my dick swinging free.

"It depends on you, quite honestly. The harder you work, the sooner you'll be discharged to go home."

Home.

Do I even have one anymore? I was staying with Jessa prior to my last deployment and I guess I'll be going back there once I'm released.

"Thanks for all your help." The corpsmen and aides here have been tremendous with all they've done for me since I woke up.

Six weeks later

Despite the scarring, I feel stronger than I have in years. I pay the cab driver, grab my bag and walk up the driveway to the house I've shared with Jessa since we started seeing one another. We dated all through high school, broke up briefly when I left for basic training, then reconnected when I came home on my first leave and have been together ever since. My dick twinges, reminding me that it's been quite some time since he got to play, and I hope that she's in the mood.

"Matt! You're home!" she exclaims as I walk in the door.

"Hey, baby, did you miss me?" I ask, putting my duffle bag down inside the door and opening my arms. She flies into them and I kiss her, pouring everything into the kiss so she realizes how much I've missed her.

"God, yes. I'm sorry I couldn't get out to see you more."

"It's okay, baby. I know you're busy with work." She's a paralegal at a big firm in town and is currently being run ragged getting information for a case they're defending.

"I've got dinner made; do you want to wash up so we can eat?"

"I'd rather have dessert," I admit, grinding my hips into her.

"Dinner can wait," she replies, holding out her hand for me. We walk into our bedroom and I take note of the subtle changes she's made since I've been gone. Nothing major; it looks like she painted and changed out the comforter set. I like it since it suits us. As we both undress, I realize that this is the moment of truth. She'll either accept me as I am, a broken, scarred man, or she'll run.

"I'm sorry, Matt," she whispers, tears running down her face while I pack my stuff. "I... I just can't. The scars being right there grosses me out. I can deal with the ones on your back." Well, la di fucking da.

I don't reply. I can't. She took one look at the scars that were near my dick and the look on her face caused me to deflate faster than a balloon that's been popped. Revulsion and disgust will kill a hard-on, that's for damn sure. Of course, since that momentous occasion last night, there's not even been a twitch so in addition to my broken body, I guess I can add a broken dick to the equation.

Once all my stuff is packed, I pull the key off my keyring and hand it to her. "Not gonna say it's okay, Jessa, because if we had already been married, those vows say for better or worse. Worse, to me, would've been coming back in a fucking box, but for you, it's the fact that I'm alive and my leg has scars that are too close to my dick. It obviously had no damage, but I won't stay with you when you look at me like I was some kind of freak."

"You're breaking our engagement?" she asks.

I can't help the bark of laughter that her question raises in me. "What the fuck do you think? My body revolts you, how the fuck do you think your actions make me feel?" I'm hurt and disappointed, sure, but there's a river of anger and rage that burns inside. I thought I knew the woman standing in front of me and to see that I had it all wrong is devastating.

"Fine. Have a nice life, Matt. For what it's worth, I am glad you're alive."

"Yeah, me too." I take the engagement ring she hands back to me, grab my duffle bag and head out the door without looking back.

It's onward and upward from here on out. The fact that I can't seem to get hard any longer fucking sucks, but I'm alive and I'll make the best of things.

I always do.

CHAPTER 1

Matt
Ten Years Later

I walk into the clubhouse and head to the bar. It's been a brutal work week with issue after issue at the construction site and I need to chill out a bit. As I drink my beer and look around, I think about how grateful I am that Reese reached out to me once I was stateside and brought me into the fold. After the shit with Jessa, I was left spinning and had no clue what I was going to do with the rest of my life. There were many nights that I stared mindlessly at my television, a bottle of Jack in one hand and my gun in the other. Something always stopped me from doing anything and as my mind drifts to the cute little waitress from The Steakhouse, I have to wonder if some higher being knew that she would come into my life.

Not that she's actually *in* my life, of course. My brothers and I see her frequently, as the restaurant is one of the club's favorites and somehow, we always get her as our waitress. She's friendly and obviously hardworking, but she doesn't do the shit that a lot of waitresses seem to do when they see a group of bikers walk into their 'domain'; she doesn't flirt, and she also doesn't seem to be scared of us just because we're bikers. I take another pull on my beer and realize that for the first time in years, I feel a twinge of desire.

I saw a therapist when I found that I couldn't get erect and he deemed that it was more of a psychological issue than a physical one, especially since, until Jessa opened her mouth, I had no problem getting hard. Regardless, no woman will want the damaged, fucked-up body I now sport, so I've pushed any thought of having a relationship deep into the recesses of my mind.

"What's going on, brother?" Reese asks as he slides onto the stool next to me and motions for a beer from one of our prospects.

"Not a helluva lot. Had a few issues today at the site, but I think it's all smoothed out now. I sure the hell hope so, anyhow."

"That's good, brother. Anything else going on that I need to be aware of?" he questions.

"Don't think so. Hey, you know that waitress?" I don't mention the nightmares that plague me every time I close my eyes, even though Reese would understand. Hell, all of my brothers would; they've all served and have the stories and scars to tell the tale.

"The one from The Steakhouse? Mandie?"

"Yeah, her."

"What's going on? Are you interested in her? Never really seen anyone catch your eye, brother."

"Fucked-up past, brother." I take a deep breath and decide that now's the time to spill it to my friend and president. He won't judge, he'd *never* judge. "When I was deployed, I was engaged." He nods but doesn't say anything in response. "Anyhow, got hurt during my last mission pretty badly and was medically discharged. She was busy with work and shit, so she wasn't really able to come see me. Had to do rehab and shit to rebuild the muscle that the injuries damaged. Finally got to come home and life went a little bit sideways."

"How so?"

"I know y'all have seen my back," I reply. "I was able to cover a lot up with tattoos thanks to a fucking awesome tat artist I found."

"Hey now, brother, what're you saying?" he asks, a smirk on his face.

"Fuck you, Reese. You know I got all of that before you tracked my ass down. No one else has inked me but you since then."

"Yeah, just fucking with you. Carry on."

This next part is going to be hard, so I motion to the prospect for a bottle of whiskey and two shot glasses. He fills them and leaves them in front of us, along with fresh beers. "You may need this," I tell him, shooting the whiskey back and motioning for another one.

"Fuck," he murmurs, before he follows suit.

"Well, what y'all don't know is the scarring extends down the left side and wraps around to the front of my thigh. Thankfully, my junk didn't get touched, but the scars are fucking gruesome. My ex couldn't handle them and said a bunch of shit that she later tried to say she didn't mean, but the damage was done. Couldn't get it up any more."

"Fuck, brother, I... I don't know what to say," he states. Yeah, that makes two of us. Here I am in the supposed prime of my life and my dick is broken. It fucking sucks, but what would be worse is if it actually worked and some woman did what Jessa did. I don't think I could handle seeing revulsion on another woman's face like I did hers.

"Not much to say, man. Saw a counselor who told me that it was in my head, but fuck, when someone sees you and says you're a monster and you can tell by the look in their eyes that they think you're repulsive, it fucks with you. Anyhow, the first person who has even gotten a rise out of me has been that waitress. No clue why either and it's not like I've done more than help her out when her car broke down. But I'm drawn to her, but what if she's like Jessa?"

Reese grabs the bottle and pours us each another shot. "Well, here's the thing and I hate feeling like a pussy saying this, but maybe it means you need to explore things with her. I understand that she's got kids; that an issue for you? Dealing with a baby daddy?"

"I don't think he's in the fucking picture. Man, the day I gave her that ride home? She had groceries and I brought them in for her. She had a loaf of bread, some peanut butter and a fucking quart of milk for her and two kids. Granted, one is still an infant from what I can tell, but Jesus, brother, I can't wrap my head around the fact that she's struggling so fucking hard."

"Sounds like another mom we have around here," he replies. "Remember how Shayla was when Nick first brought her around?"

I nod. She was so hesitant to take any help and had left an abusive situation to wind up living in her van with her little girl. It wasn't until Nick stepped in and got her to his family that her life started to change. Now, they're married with another little one on the way. "So what you're saying is I need to see where things go."

"Absolutely. Let me know if you need our help, brother."

"Will do." I push back the empties and with a slap on the back, head up to my room.

Mandie

Another shift, another fifty dollars to tuck away toward next month's bills. I sigh as I head out to my car, exhaustion hitting me square between the eyes. At least my babysitter doesn't charge too much and she watches the kids at my house, so I don't have to worry about driving her home. Plus, she's old enough to drive and I always have her text me when she arrives home, so I don't worry about her being out at night. I'll take those little blessings wherever I can find them, that's for damn sure. Before I head to the house, I stop at the grocery store, coupons in hand, and pick up a few things. Something has to give soon because I've lost so much weight that I look like a skeleton with skin stretched over my body. I'm waiting to see if I get approved for food stamps, but there's been an influx of new applicants according to the caseworker who did my telephone interview, and they're backed up. Regardless, my babies need food and I can and will suck it up. I'm grateful that Juan, our cook and the owner of the restaurant, manages to slip me the occasional meal because he's 'made too much' and he doesn't 'want it to go to waste'. He doesn't push too much, probably because he knows my pride won't let me take it, but I get at least one meal every shift and since I've survived on less, I consider myself fortunate. Best thing I ever did was get a job at The Steakhouse. They've helped me so much, especially now that I'm almost done with college. My schedule is late-week intensive, but during the earlier part of the week, I take shifts during the day so I can do my classwork online at night. The tips aren't as good, but again, Juan and his wife, Maria, do what they can to take care of me.

Once I've paid for my meager purchases, I carry them out to my car and put them in the trunk before heading home. I smile when my car cranks right up. Even though I haven't seen him since, the night that Matt found me after my car broke down was a lifesaver. When my car was returned, it had been tuned up, gassed up, and I found a phone card with minutes in the console with a note to 'use them'. I tried to find out how much my car repairs cost and was told that the club had handled them, even the four brand-new tires and new brakes. Despite the age of my vehicle, it runs as good as if it were brand-new.

When I arrive home, I head into the house and see Olive, the babysitter, feeding the kids. "Hey, Olive," I say as I maneuver into the kitchen with the three bags of food.

"Hey, Mandie. How was your day?" she asks, blowing raspberries at Beau so he'll eat.

"It was okay, I guess. They give you any problems?" I question.

"Are you kidding me? They're good as gold, Mandie. Oh! I uh, I started a garden in the backyard. I hope that's okay with you. Mom bought too many seed packets and said they wouldn't be good next year, so I figured what the hell."

I smile at her. "Fresh vegetables? Absolutely. They're so damn expensive right now."

"Anything I can do to help," she states. "You good to take over?"

"Absolutely. I'll pay you this weekend when I get my check."

"I know you're good for it, my friend." She kisses both of the kids, gives me a hug, then heads out the door, leaving me with the two best things I've ever done.

"How are Momma's babies today?" I ask.

"We played, Momma," Aria replies. "Beau ate dirt."

I laugh because I can see the evidence of his adventure in gardening all over his face and body. While some may think I'm a bad mother for letting my kids get dirty, I found out long ago it was easier to pick my battles. Olive made sure his face and hands were clean before she started feeding him, knowing I'll give him a bath. Aria doesn't look too bad, but she's getting to an age where she acts like a little girl, and she no longer likes getting her hands dirty.

"It's okay, sweetie. Sometimes boys do that. Did you have enough to eat? If you did, I have popsicles for dessert." They're the cheap, no-name ones, but my kids don't care. She nods, so I grab the empty plates and put them in the sink before I get two popsicles out and hand one to her while I hold Beau's to his face so he can enjoy the frozen treat.

"That can't be right," I murmur, looking at my school-issued laptop. It's something else I'm thankful for because otherwise, I would've had to figure out how to go in for classes. Instead, I've been able to do the majority of it online. The best part is once I graduate, if my grade point average remains high enough, the laptop becomes mine. "There's no way I should have that much left over from my grant." I look again and sure enough, after my tuition for my last class is paid, I have five hundred dollars. My mind spins as I think about what I can get paid and how I can maybe get a little bit ahead for a change. Ever since Alistair left, I've been living hand to mouth. I think back to that fateful day and while it's been a struggle, I'd rather do that than deal with his fucked-up ass.

"I can't believe you got pregnant again, Mandie," he growled out, throwing his beer across the room. He's drunk. Again. Of course, since he lost his latest job, that seemed to be his constant state. I probably should have waited to tell him I was pregnant, but he pushed the issue when he wanted to know why I wasn't drinking.

"It's not like I did it alone, Alistair," I retorted. I'm so pissed at his attitude that I completely missed the back-hand he sent my way until my head bounced off the wall. Before I could say anything, he was on me, his fists punching anywhere he could reach while I struggled to stay conscious and protect my face and stomach. At least Aria was asleep.

"I'm out of here, you worthless cunt. Have a nice life," he sneered as he aimed his fist at my face again, knocking me out. When I regained consciousness, it was because I heard Aria crying, so I painfully made my way to her bedroom to see her soaking wet.

I shake my head to let the old memories go. It wasn't easy being alone, but I found the job at The Steakhouse despite being pregnant and started college classes so that I could make a better life for me and my kids. When Juan introduced me to his daughter, Olive, I thought I'd died and gone to Heaven. She's been a godsend to me and my kids and for a teenager, she's pretty level-headed. The money she lets me pay her goes to her clothes fund, as she calls it. Grabbing my notebook, I start jotting down things I need; both kids have outgrown most of their clothes so that'll be the first order of business, especially since it's getting warmer. Aria's fourth birthday is also coming up, so I need to put some of the money back for that as well. I spend a consider-able amount of time crossing through things and adding others until I have a plan. Maybe this is just the thing I need so that I can breathe easy for a little while.

CHAPTER 2

Matt

I can't get the thought of Reese's words about Mandie out of my head as I leave the construction site for the day. It's Friday and I know she'll be working, so I head to the store and start shopping. Once I've gotten everything I think she and two little kids will like, I grab a few coolers and some ice, pack it all inside to keep it from spoiling, then head toward her house.

There's a single light on inside as well as the one on the porch. Once again, I notice that the deck is in dire need of repair and make a mental note to come by in the daytime to see what I can do. I've got plenty of scraps that will be sufficient to fix the broken boards. I don't question why this is important to me as I haul the coolers and bags of groceries up onto her deck. Once I have everything situated, I head back to my truck and point it in the direction of the clubhouse.

We've got our typical Friday night party going on and even though we're not the kind of club to have whores hanging around, it seems as though every available female from around town is here tonight. I've said 'no thanks' to quite a few and received glares for my effort. What can I say? None of them have caused any sort of physical reaction so why bother. Not only that, but I'm positive that if they saw my scars, they'd run screaming from the room. The only thing that seems to get me hard, even minimally, are thoughts of Mandie.

"You doing okay, brother?" Nick asks as he comes up to the table I'm sitting at, his service dog, Bosco, at his side. Once he sits down and passes me a fresh beer, I notice that Bosco positions himself closer to me.

"Yeah, just observing," I mutter before opening up the new bottle and taking a swig. "Seems like there are a lot of new faces here tonight."

"I noticed that," he says. "Hey, not to get into your business or anything, brother, but I was wondering if you've ever thought about getting a dog for yourself."

"A dog?"

"Shit, okay, so I know you have nightmares. I had them too and since I got my boy, they're not as often."

"How do you know I have nightmares?" It's not something I've shared with my brothers – the fact that when I'm asleep, my men visit me. The faces change but one thing never does; they're always covered in blood. So much so that it flows from them onto the ground. There have been a few times when I've woken up that I half expect to see puddles of crimson red around my bed.

He looks down at his bottle then back at me. "I've heard you screaming a few times, Matt. When we've stayed here at the clubhouse after a late night." His voice is low and almost apologetic.

"Fuck, I'm sorry. Don't mean to wake anyone up because I have them," I reply, guilt swamping me at the thought I'm keeping my brother awake at night.

"I was already awake. I still get them like I said. Not as bad as before Bosco, because when they hit, he crowds me until the feelings pass, but that's the thing about PTSD. We never know when it's going to strike and rear its ugly head. Anyhow, we've got a few dogs at the sanctuary and I think they're trainable if you're interested."

I think about what he's saying. For the most part, during the day, I'm fine. Sometimes, a loud noise at the site will have me dropping to the ground, but I'm getting better about it the longer time passes. "That might not be a bad idea," I state. "It sure as fuck can't hurt." Plus, with what I do, I can always take the dog with me to work.

"Good. Whenever you're available, let me know and we'll meet over there."

"Appreciate it, brother." I'm about to say something else when his woman, Shayla, comes over and plops onto his lap.

"Can we go to The Steakhouse tomorrow night, Nick?" she asks. My ears perk up because with it being the weekend, I know Mandie will be working. Now how do I finagle an invitation?

"Don't see why not. Maybe we should see if anyone else wants to go," he says, giving me a look. I flip him off behind Shayla's back and he smirks at me. Fucker.

"Awesome! Me, Corrie, and Kirsten want to see when Mandie graduates. Corrie said she found out that she'll get her accounting degree and she wants to talk to her about maybe doing the books for the sanctuary from home so she can stay with her kids."

"Then it's settled," Nick states. "Who knows, maybe we can have her do all of our books. Anything to give her a hand; I know she's likely struggling." I'm positive of that fact, having witnessed first-hand myself how she's living hand to mouth. Gotta give her credit, however; despite the fact that she probably pinches her pennies so tight they give change, she's always upbeat and outgoing.

"What time do you think?" Shayla questions, looking at Nick. "Should we go kind of early?" He leans in and whispers something in her ear and I watch her turn a pretty shade of pink, so I know whatever he said was meant for her ears only.

Damn, I want that kind of intimate relationship with someone. I thought I had that with Jessa, but I was obviously mistaken.

Maybe Mandie...

"Matt? Will five work for you?" Shayla asks, interrupting my thoughts.

"Yeah, it's a short day tomorrow which'll give me time to get cleaned up," I reply.

"Then it's settled. I'll call in the morning and make a reservation and tell them we want to be put in Mandie's section," Shayla states. She leans in and kisses Nick then bounces off, likely to go find Corrie and Kirsten.

"Does she ever slow down?" I inquire, sipping my beer.

"Not really. For someone who had no clue what being part of this life was about, she's taken to it like a duck to water." I chuckle because once she was brought into the family, she embraced it with both hands. The three old ladies we have here have shown me time and again that my relationship with Jessa was sorely lacking.

"Well, you've got a good old lady, brother," I remark. Looking around, I see that the party is gearing up and with what I have going on in the morning, I decide to cut my losses and head up to my room. "I'll see y'all tomorrow at the restaurant. Early day."

"Goodnight, brother."

"Goodnight, Nick. I'll let you know when I can come out and see what you've got."

"Any day is good, just hit me up." I nod before I grab my empty bottle, toss it into the recycling bin, then motion for the prospect to give me another.

Once in my room, I strip out of my clothes and head into my shower. As the hot water soothes my tired muscles, I drink my beer and think about Mandie, as well as getting a dog to help me with my PTSD. I wonder if she's gotten home yet and seen what I did. Not that I left a note or anything; that's not my style. In fact, I'll probably never tell her it was me. But I make a mental note to stop by the bank and grab some cash out of the ATM to give her a tip tomorrow night. We tip pretty well, but ever since the first time I met her, I've always given her extra in cash.

I finish my shower, shave, then once I'm done with my beer, brush my teeth before I slip on a pair of boxer briefs and slide into bed. Grabbing my remote, I queue up a new show on Netflix that I started the other day. I've found that having the television on seems to help a little with keeping my nightmares at bay.

Mandie

Exhaustion follows me to my car. We had three back-to-back groups and I was run off my feet most of the night. Despite the excellent service that I gave them, along with a new waitress who I am mentoring, two of the groups left a whopping five-dollar tip. Considering that the bill for the first party was over three hundred dollars and the second group spent almost five hundred dollars,

I feel cheated. At least Juan pays his waitstaff minimum wage instead of what a lot of folks in this industry get, but still, if a group is going to spend that kind of money on food and drinks, they could at least tip their servers appropriately. I suspect it was because a few of the men were flirting with the new girl.

Juan pulled me aside after they left and asked how we made out and when I told him, he shook his head then checked the ticket to see if maybe they had put one on their card. He doesn't usually add an automatic gratuity to large groups because his restaurant is upscale enough that it's never been an issue before. He tried to give me some money from his own pocket, but I refused it and told him I'd be fine.

As I drive home, I think about the errands I need to run with the kids in the morning. First, I need to get them some clothes, then we'll do a good grocery shop with the extra money left from my tuition grant. I can stock up on non-perishable items and stuff for my deep freezer that should hold me and the kids over for a bit.

When I pull into my driveway, I see things on my deck. "What on earth?" I murmur to myself as I park my car and get out. Stepping up on the deck, I see several coolers, as well as a bunch of bags. I carefully open one cooler and am shocked to see packs of chicken, roasts, pork chops, and ground beef. When I open the second one, I see easy frozen meals packed in ice. I examine the bags and find cans of soup, SpaghettiOs, ravioli; all things the kids love. There are boxes of cereal, macaroni and cheese, several loaves of bread, peanut butter and jelly, vegetables. "Who could have done this for us?" I wonder.

I unlock the door and see Olive sleeping on the couch, so I carefully start carrying the bags in, then drag the coolers inside and toward the kitchen. "What's all of that?" Olive asks, her voice husky with sleep.

"I was going to ask you the same thing. I found it all on the deck when I got home. You don't know who did it?"

"Not a clue," she says. "Here, let me help you get this put up. You look dead on your feet."

"It was a long night, that's for sure," I reply. "I can't believe this, it's like Christmas or something."

"I don't think I've ever seen this much food in your house at one time," Olive admits.

My shoulders sag at her words. "I'm failing, aren't I?" I whisper as tears fall down my face. She rushes over and throws her arms around me.

"No, you're not. The kids have everything they need. You've got a roof over your head and food for y'alls bellies. You're doing the best you possibly can, Mandie, and I won't let you talk about my friend like you're doing." Her words make me giggle and soon, we're both laughing as we continue stocking my cabinets, freezer, and fridge.

"With what we grow in the garden, I'll be able to get through without worrying too much until I find a job once I graduate," I tell her. "Of course, I'll still work The Steakhouse on the weekends."

"When will you spend time with the kids if you're working all the time?"

I sigh. "I don't know. I just know I have to save money and if that means I have to work two jobs for a bit, that's what I'll do."

"You're a good mom, Mandie," she states, her face serious. "You took a shitty situation and have worked your ass off to make something out of nothing."

"There are days I wonder, Olive," I whisper. "Days like today, before I got home, when a large party stiffed me on a decent tip." I swear, even though she's seventeen going on eighteen, she's got an old soul.

"Why did they do that?" she asks. I can tell she's upset on my behalf based on the look that crosses her face.

"I'm training a new girl, which is fine. Your folks have me do that quite frequently since I know the menu inside and out, as well as the way they like things done. However, I think a few of the women in two of the groups took exception to the fact that she was kind of flirty with their men."

"Did you tell my dad?"

"Yeah, I did. Your dad is something, Ollie. He tried to give me money from his own damn wallet to make up for them not tipping me, but I wouldn't let him do it! Y'all have all done more than enough for me and the kids."

"We've only done what you have let us do, Mandie. If you'd let us, we'd do so much more."

"I can't," I whisper. "It's not a pride thing, either. It's just how I was raised, and I know if I work hard enough, I'll get out of this situation that I found myself in after he left."

"Shit, that man was useless to begin with and everyone knows that."

I nod because apparently, I was the last to know just how awful Alistair McAdams was and once again, I'm grateful we didn't get married and that the kids don't have his name, even though they're both his. I honestly think I was so afraid that I'd never find anyone to love me that I latched onto the first person who showed me any attention. The joke was on me, though, because after his treatment of me, I doubt I'll ever let anyone get that close to me again.

"Thanks for all your help, Ollie. Here, I've got your money," I tell her, going to my purse and pulling out several bills.

"Maybe you should hang onto it since tonight was so sparse," she says, trying to hand it back to me.

"Nope. With all of this, plus the extra that was left over from my tuition grant, I'll be fine, sweetie. You take this; you've earned it and so much more." She hugs me and I relish the fact that this young lady is in my life. I'm blessed, that's for damn sure.

CHAPTER 3

Matt

"Hey, brother, you got time to meet me at the sanctuary now?" I ask Nick when he answers his phone.

"Absolutely. I can be there in twenty."

"Then I'll see you there." I disconnect the call and toss my phone into the cupholder. Despite falling asleep to thoughts of Mandie, I woke up covered in sweat, cowering in the corner, with the vague memories of Jackal standing over me dripping blood and asking me 'Why?' over and over. I had no answer when it happened and despite the decade that has passed, I still have no answer as to why we were targeted that fateful day.

Needless to say, I wasn't in the right frame of mind to do a lot on the job site today, but I pushed through anyhow so that the inspector could come out on Monday and sign off on that phase of the project. We get a bonus if we get it finished in time and some shitty weather early on put us a bit behind. Thankfully, we've gotten caught up because my crew thrives on a challenge.

I swing by a fast food restaurant and grab a burger and a drink and eat while driving out to the sanctuary that Reese's old lady, Corrie, started. It's still one of the projects I'm proudest of being a part of because we incorporated the natural landscape, as well as huge boulders I brought in from a commercial construction site, to give the animals who live there a shot at a normal life, even if they never get adopted.

When I pull in, I see Nick standing there talking to Corrie and Reese. I don't feel ganged up on though; these are my brothers and they only have my well-being in mind. "Hey, brothers, Corrie," I say as I get out of my truck.

"Hey, Matt! I had to come when Nick mentioned you wanted to get a dog," Corrie replies.

"And since we were running errands without the kids, I came along as well," Reese supplies, a smirk on his face. I discreetly flip him off because I'm sure they made a trip by the clubhouse sans kids based on Corrie's wild hair, something I won't remark on because I'd die before embarrassing her.

"Gotcha," I state, smirking back. His smirk widens and I have to hold back the laughter that wants to come out. "Where are these dogs?" I ask Nick.

"Follow me," he commands, chuckling. We walk through several gates and I spy a lot of the older senior dogs sunning themselves on the rocks we got from one construction project, while others frolic in the small pools of water me and my crew built. As we approach one section, I see several dogs standing at attention and instinctively know that these are the dogs who Nick thinks will be trainable for someone like me.

"What do I need to do?" It's been years since I've had a dog and the ones I had growing up were working dogs, not pets. Although, I guess the one I get would also be a working dog.

"Honestly? Just sit somewhere and get comfortable. What I've noticed is that one will gravitate to you if you're patient." I nod and prepare to settle in for a while, grateful that I thought to grab my drink. I notice that Corrie and Reese didn't follow us; they went into the barn where the feral cats live. Nick, however, sits down near me and we start chatting about inconsequential things.

I watch as the dogs come closer, their noses in the air. Long minutes pass until one that looks like a cross between a border collie and a lab comes even closer before he sits in front of me, his tail wagging and head tilted. "That's Champ," Nick says as he watches the dog watch me. "I've already started working with him so if you like him, he's good to go. He's up to date on all his shots and has been neutered as well."

"Hey, Champ," I whisper. His head tilts again and he moves even closer until his nose is touching my hand. "How you doing, boy?" His tail wags harder and I feel his tongue lick my fingers. "You're a handsome fella, aren't you?" I've never seen coloring like his before, and his eyes are cool; I don't think I've ever seen a dog with two different colored eyes before.

"He's a tri-colored border collie. I know he looks like he's got some lab in him, but we rescued him and his parents from a hoarding situation. In fact, he's got papers, although I doubt that matters much to you."

"Doesn't mean shit to me, brother," I reply, rubbing my hand through Champ's fur. "His eyes are cool, too."

"He's definitely a unique looking dog, that's for damn sure. And he's almost freakishly smart. I don't think you're going to have any issues with him, but we can work together to make sure he knows what he needs to do." I'm fine with that but already I notice that the stress that was hanging over me from my shitty night has significantly abated.

"Alright, let's do this. What do I need to get food-wise? Anything special?"

"Follow me. Go ahead and call him so he gets used to you giving him commands, brother."

"Champ, come," I state. Champ stands and without any fuss, comes alongside so he's almost touching me, and we walk back through the gates until we're at the small building where Corrie handles all the paperwork. I see she and Reese are standing there and notice she's got a folder in her hand and that Reese has a huge bag of dog food over his shoulder.

"Your first bag of food is on us," Corrie says when I go to question her as to what they're doing. "This folder has all of his shot records, his rabies certification, and his microchip information. You'll need to go online to update that with your personal stuff; right now, he's registered to the sanctuary."

"How much?" I question. I'm also wondering how she knew which dog I'd choose, but knowing her, she had a feeling. It's part of the reason why the sanctuary has been so successful with the adoption events. She and her vet friend, Jeanette, instinctively seem to know which animals will be best paired with the families that show up.

"Uh, just saying, but no Black Tuxedos MC brother will *ever* pay a penny to adopt one of these guys," Corrie emphatically states. "In fact, no one who has served our country will. That's why I have grants, Matt."

"Then I'll make a donation," I reply.

"I won't take it," she retorts.

"Is she always this stubborn?" I ask Reese. "I don't think I ever noticed that about her before."

"You won't win this one, brother," he says.

"Then I've got y'alls dinner tonight. It's the least I can do." Especially if Champ helps me get through the night.

"Fine, I'll accept that. Enjoy your new life, Champ. I'm sure I'll see you around."

"You can count on it since I live at the clubhouse. Plus, I'm planning on him going with me to work so I have company."

"That should work."

"Thanks again. I'll see y'all in a few hours. Need to get back and get cleaned up before tonight."

"See you there, brother," Reese states. I raise my hand as I head to my truck and when I open the door, Champ jumps inside and moves over to the passenger side before he sits down and looks at me.

"Welcome to my life, Champ," I whisper as I get into the truck and get turned around to head back to the clubhouse. "Let's see if we can do this thing."

Mandie

Today's shopping was definitely less expensive than I originally anticipated thanks to the amazing good Samaritan who dropped off all the food. As I fold laundry, I smile when I think of how Maria, Juan's wife, called me this morning to tell me that a local church was having their semi-annual kid's consignment sale. Olive came over and together, we took the kids and loaded them up with virtually brand-new wardrobes for a fraction of the money I thought I'd spend. I can now tuck more money back for a rainy day. It's not much, but in my experience, every little bit counts.

"You should probably go rest for a bit since you have to work tonight," Olive says, coming into the laundry room.

"Yeah, that's not a bad idea. No clue what tonight will bring, that's for sure." With the kids taking a nap, I don't have to worry about them, so I head to my room and strip down to my underwear before I slide beneath the covers. I set my alarm even though I know that Olive won't let me oversleep.

As I drift off to sleep, a certain biker crosses my thoughts.

Walking into The Steakhouse, I immediately notice that it's packed again. Hopefully that means I'll leave with a lot of tips. I clock in and grab my apron, grateful that despite the fact that we're an upscale restaurant, because we're in Texas, jeans are part of our uniform. We have cute polo-style shirts with the logo on the left side and have a black apron we wear around our waists with our order pad and pens inside. "You've got a party that specifically requested you," Shona says once I've clocked in. "I also gave you the surrounding tables; let me know if you want some help."

I'm already shaking my head. I don't need the new girl working with me tonight to fuck up my tips. She already did that last night and while I have a tiny nest egg now, I want to add to it because we're coming up on the time of year when Aria's asthma tends to flare up. "I think I'll be good, Shona, but thanks. Do you know who the party is?" I inquire.

"Those bikers. Y'know, the guys and their women from the Black Tuxedos?" I feel the smile gracing my face as I nod at her. I love it when they come in; they're a fun group and despite the fact that they're bikers, they're relatively easy-going, all things considered. The first time they came in and I served them, I was a nervous wreck because I'd never been around bikers. Yet, despite the fact that the guys are huge, and most are sporting tattoos, they've always been good to me.

"Awesome. I really like them. Best customers I've ever had," I confess.

"Really? It doesn't bother you that they're kind of rough looking?" My face crunches up at her words; their hair may be longer than society deems appropriate, but other than that, they treat everyone they come in contact with while here with respect. Not only that, but all of them are former military and that means a lot to me.

"Uh, no. In fact, I think some of them are kind of hot," I admit, thinking of Matt. While thoughts of him are nothing more than a fantasy, given my past, I can't help the fact that he crosses my mind more often than not.

"Huh, didn't take you for one of those girls," she murmurs. My hackles raise, and I find myself jumping to their defense.

"What do you mean by that?" I question.

"Well, you know, women who fall at a biker's feet, you're one of those."

I can almost feel the steam coming out of my ears. I'm so livid right now I'm shaking. "Shona, you don't know me or my history, so I'll let that comment slide for now. However, that being said, you're being extremely judgmental about a group of people who have businesses in our community, do a lot for our town, and have always, *always* been supporters of this place, ever since Juan opened it. I think you need to check yourself." Okay, so the slang may be out of date, but right now, I don't give that first fuck. These people are my friends, kind of anyway, and I won't allow anyone to demean them.

Shona starts to say something and is interrupted by Juan. "Shona, I think you need an early night tonight. Go ahead and clock out, we'll handle it." I glance at him and judging by the firm set of his jaw and the fact his arms are crossed over his burly chest, I know he heard most if not all of what she said.

"Juan, we're really busy. I didn't mean anything by it."

"Shona, here's the thing. I'm a third generation Mexican American married to a black woman who has Native American ancestry. I've dealt with people casting aspersions on me as well as my family most of my life and vowed that I would take my mother's teachings to heart. She always told me to treat others the way I wanted to be treated, to look at what a person does, not what they say, and to never judge them by their appearance because good comes in all packages, as does bad. Those men and women have hearts of gold and have done more for this town than any person who's ever been tasked to run it. Not only that, but each of the men served our country, which tells me more about their character than anything else, including the fact that they like to ride Harleys and wear their hair longer. Now, clock out. I think you need to reflect on your attitude to see if you are, in fact, a good fit here."

She stomps off after clocking out, leaving me alone with Juan. I look at him and with tears in my eyes say, "I don't understand how people can treat each other badly based on the color of their skin, especially in this day and age. You, Maria, and Olive have been such a godsend and a blessing in my life that I consider you family."

"You're family to us as well, Mandie. You and those adorable babies of yours. Sadly, I don't think it'll ever change, but what makes it bearable most days is the fact that the majority of the people we come in contact with are not like Shona. And truthfully, the fact of the matter is, that's what most are taught growing up. It doesn't make it right but some day, hopefully in my lifetime, it'll change."

"I hope so, Juan. Okay, I better get to work, or you won't have a restaurant to run because folks will leave," I state. He laughs at me and pulls me in for a quick hug.

"You just keep being you, Mandie. I know you got a rough deal growing up, but what we, Maria and I, have seen since you came here is a woman determined to forge her own way. Just remember, it's okay to accept a helping hand every now and again. Now scoot."

I nod and pull away to head out to the dining area. Time to get to work.

I quickly get the other two tables squared away while I wait for the Black Tuxedos to show up, since they made a reservation. When my heart rate accelerates, I know that he's here. Matt. The man who fuels all my late-night fantasies. Considering how nasty Alistair was to me, I'm surprised that I have any feelings for a man. After he beat me half to death then left, it took me a few weeks to recover and by the time I did, I was down to my last few dollars. I still remember walking into The Steakhouse, Aria in tow because I didn't have a babysitter at the time only to come face-to-face with Juan.

"You need something, little one?" the gruff-voiced man asked me.

"I need a job, sir. I'm hard working and dependable, but I need to work so I can feed my daughter," I replied.

He gave me an appraising look and I found myself standing as tall as possible. Granted, at five-feet-three-

inches, that wasn't very impressive, but I needed to work. I gave Aria the last of the oatmeal this morning and drank water to stave off my own hunger pains. I was able to get a bag of nonperishables from the food pantry, but that won't last long, and I needed to eat to make sure that my baby was healthy. "When can you start?" he questioned.

"As soon as you need me. I have to find a babysitter, but that shouldn't be a problem." I could always check with my old Sunday school teacher to see if she would help me, at least until I found someone else.

"My daughter can watch her for you. Ollie!" he shouted. I watched as a teenager, who is shorter than me, came out to stand next to her father.

"Si, Papa," she said.

"I am hiring her," he stated, pointing at me. "You will watch her little one, si?"

She looked at me and then Aria before she broke out into a smile. "I'd love to. Where do I watch her? Here? Your house?"

"My house would probably be better at some point, since it has all of her things."

"Okay, I'll need your address then. Oh, and maybe y'alls names?"

I giggled because she was almost bouncing on her feet with excitement. "I'm Mandie, Mandie Matchum, and this little cutie is Aria. Aria, can you say hello to Miss Ollie?"

"Hi, Owwee," Aria lisped out.

"Oh my God, she's adorable. Come here, sweet girl," Ollie said. I handed over my daughter who was reaching out for her new babysitter. With my arms now free, I reached into my purse for the pad and paper I always carried.

"Um, I don't have a spare key right now, but I'll get another one made just for you if that's okay. Is it a problem if you watched her at your house until I got one and could show you around my house?" I questioned. I mean, I had a good feeling about her, but I don't know her yet and definitely needed to be protective as far as letting just anyone into my home.

"That's fine. I know when the restaurant closes, and I also know that my papa won't keep his waitstaff here late. That's what the night crew is for, right, Papa?" she inquired.

He chuckled at his daughter before nodding. "Mandie, follow me so I can get paperwork on you and get you started."

I'm brought out of my memories when I hear, "Hey, Mandie!" Turning, I see Reese's wife, Corrie, walking over toward me.

"Hey, Corrie. How are y'all tonight?" I ask as I motion for them to follow me. I don't miss the fact that Matt watching me, or how that makes me feel inside. It still blows my mind a little that I sense whenever he's near; we've spoken in the past, of course, but we've never had what I would consider an in-depth conversation or anything. Even the night he gave me a ride home when my car broke down, we kept it somewhat superficial.

There's something about him and I wish life were different for me so I could pursue him. But no man wants to take on a woman with two kids, so I push that fantasy deep into the recesses of my mind.

"We're good. Ready for some of the best steak Texas has to offer," she replies as they start sitting down.

"Do y'all know what you'd like to drink? I can go grab those for y'all while you check out the specials," I state, pulling out my pad and pen. I know there are waitresses who memorize everything, and I do that as well, but having it written down helps keep me organized. I go around the table and take down their drink orders then leave to get them prepared. "I'll be back in a few. If you have any questions about the specials, let me know when I return."

As I hurry back to the drink station, I can feel Matt's eyes burning a hole in my back and wonder if maybe, possibly, he's feeling the same attraction as I am.

Once I return with their drinks, I again go around the table, answering questions about the specials and taking their dinner orders. On my way to the kitchen to turn them in, I stop by my other two tables and get requests for drink refills from one couple and for the check at the second table.

I continue taking care of my large party, even as the other two tables finally clear out, are cleaned and then reset. I notice that no one has been put in my section and after refilling the drinks for my bikers, I head off to search for Juan. "Juan? I know we're busy, do you want to put someone in my section? They're just about done with their meal and while I know they'll have dessert based on past history with them, I can handle it."

"You had a rough night last night, Mandie, with those huge parties who ran you ragged. I think you deserve an easy night and knowing Reese and his crew, you'll more than make up for it on your tips." I nod because they always take care of me. Hell, I've seen Reese go up to the bar and tip the bartender directly for the mixed drinks that Corrie prefers.

"Thanks, Juan. Just remember, the offer is open."

"I think we're good until they leave, honey girl." My face warms at his endearment; he and his wife, Maria, are always doing that to me and it makes me remember my mom. She died when I was barely a teenager and I went into the foster care system. I was fortunate, however, because I got a phenomenal woman for a foster mother in Mama T.

I nod and head back over to the table and grin when I see the women with their heads together, perusing the dessert menu. "I kind of figured y'all would want dessert," I say as heads pop up to look at me. "Anything in particular tonight?"

"We want it all," Nick's wife, Shayla, murmurs, glancing back down at the glossy dessert menu.

Glancing around the table, I mentally recall the past orders they've had. With the actual size of the desserts, they could probably get away ordering one of each and there would be plenty for everyone to share. "How about if I bring y'all one of each except the Death by Chocolate; I'll bring two of them, along with extra plates and clean forks. That way, you can share."

"One of those chocolate things is mine, do you hear me?" Corrie retorts, looking around the table. "The last time, I barely got a bite. Maybe we should get three of the Death by Chocolate."

"Mandie, make it three of the chocolate things so my woman gets her fix, and one of each of the others, plus a carafe of coffee," Reese states.

I start to turn away when Corrie asks, "When will you be done with college? Are you going to try and find a bookkeeping position or something?"

"I'd like to, yes," I reply.

"I may have a proposition for you if you have a few minutes to talk?" she questions.

"Sure, let me put in the dessert order and I'll come right back. Does anyone need anything else to drink besides coffee?" Everyone shakes their head, so I nod and head to the kitchen to put in their order once I've keyed it into their master bill.

"Juan, can someone bring it out when it's ready? They'll need extra plates and forks," I query. "Corrie asked about my plans once I graduate and said she has a proposition to run by me."

"I'll take care of it for you personally," he states, giving me a wink.

I carry back a carafe of coffee, along with creamer. Thankfully, when we set the tables, we put out coffee cups and the sweeteners are in a small tin pail on the table itself. Once I have everyone's coffee poured, I stand there and wait. I can feel Matt's eyes on me, assessing every move, but I don't dare glance in his direction. I feel very vulnerable right now and as broken as I am, I can't let him know I'm interested.

"Okay, so here's the thing. We have a CPA for the tax bullshit, but I can't keep up with the paperwork that he needs for the sanctuary. Is that something you could do? You'd be responsible for issuing invoices, paying vendors for supplies, that kind of thing. Plus, making sure that everything is current so when the CPA goes in to pull his reports, he can do it quickly."

"Yes, I can." This would be a major blessing for me. It would be a steadier income than I get at the restaurant, for the most part. Actually, my paychecks vary slightly as I have the same schedule each week. The only thing that really fluctuates are the tips, which I use for groceries. *But you don't have to worry about that for a little while,* my conscience supplies.

"Sweet! Okay, can you give me your number? What I'm looking for can be done remotely for the most part; you'd just have to come by the sanctuary to pick up the invoices that need to be paid. In fact, we can set up an office at your house and maybe one of the prospects can bring the mail over daily. You can print out the checks and get them ready to send out as needed and he can bring them to me to sign and drop off at the post office. It's a win-win! You'll be able to be home with your babies," she enthusiastically states.

I feel like I must have died and gone to Heaven right now as I scribble down my phone number just as Juan arrives with a tray heaping with desserts, plates and extra silverware. I quickly gather the empty plates so he has room, then place each dessert in the middle of the table except one, which I set right in front of Corrie. Her giggle makes me laugh and soon, the whole room is ringing with our laughter. Even Matt, who is usually so quiet, is laughing.

Don't think about how handsome he looks when he smiles, I chant to myself.

At long last, they've finished their meal and the table has been cleared by the busboy by the time I return with the check and several to-go boxes for the leftover desserts. Matt hands me his card and indicates it's for the whole bill so I nod then go to take care of it so they can all get on with their night. I bring over the receipt for him to sign, along with a pen that I know he won't steal seeing as it has a bright pink pompom on the top. "Thanks for coming in tonight, y'all. I hope you enjoyed your meals. Corrie, I'm off tomorrow if you want to call me."

"I'll do that, but I won't call early. Hopefully your munchkins will allow you to sleep in a little bit," she says.

"Yeah, that'll never happen. Aria will sleep as long as possible. Beau, on the other hand? He's up with the roosters. At least he still naps," I admit.

As I head back toward the area where we pull drinks and input food orders, I feel Matt behind me. Turning, I look at him and ask, "Is there something I can get you,

Matt?" I know I gave him his credit card back, along with the receipt, so I can't figure out why he would intentionally seek me out.

"This is for you, too," he replies, holding up a bunch of folded bills.

"You already tipped me for y'alls bill, you don't need to do this as well," I say.

"Please, take it," he implores. I instinctively know that he's not the type of man who begs for anything, so I take the money and slide it into my apron pocket.

"Thank you," I murmur. "Y'all are always so good to me."

"You deserve every good thing, Mandie."

"How can you say something like that? You don't really know me, Matt," I retort.

"I'd like to change that," he admits.

I shake my head at his words; I must be hearing things because there's no way on God's green earth that a man like him would be interested in me, a woman with two kids and no family.

"Yeah there is, sweetheart," he emphatically states.

"I said that out loud, didn't I?" I question. I know my face is redder than old man Johnson's barn right now. I'm an idiot, plain and simple.

His chuckle sends shivers coursing through me and I peer through my hands which cover my eyes. I see the warmth in his gaze and when he gently pulls my hands away so we're looking at one another with no barrier, he leans in closer and says, "I want to know everything there is to know about you, Mandie Matchum." His husky voice touches a part of my soul that I didn't know was there. I can feel myself instinctively moving closer, seeking out the safety of his embrace.

"You do?" I whisper. He nods, never breaking our eye contact. "I don't know what to say," I admit. My relationship with Alistair was borne out of necessity; we both aged out of the foster care system and decided that two against the world was better than one.

"Say yes, Mandie. There's something about you, about the connection I feel toward you that I want to explore."

"If you're sure, then yes. I-I will admit that I'm nervous."

"Why? Is it because of the club?" I see his eyes darken and reach out to touch his hand.

"No! It's because my past is ugly, and I don't know how much I have to offer anyone, and I think you deserve nothing but the best."

"I'm looking at her right now," he insists, taking my hand in his. "Do you feel this?" he asks, placing my hand against his chest. I can feel his heart pounding beneath his shirt, the warmth seeping into my hand. "I've been drawn to you since the first time I saw you, Mandie."

"I've been drawn to you too," I confess. "I just never thought anything would come of it, given my situation."

"Well, you thought wrong. Since tomorrow is Sunday, I want to come over and fix your deck for you."

"I can't let you spend money like that, Matt. You and the club already fixed my car!" Something I'm still a bit upset about because they wouldn't accept any money toward the repairs, and I know it was significant.

"It's not a big deal, sweetheart. I have material left over from various jobs that I'll be using, but I want you to have something that's safe. You and the kids deserve that much."

"If you're sure, then I accept," I reply, remembering Juan's words that it's okay to take a helping hand every now and then.

"I'll be there around ten in the morning if that's okay with you. That way, you'll have time to get up and take care of the kids."

"Thank you, Matt. I feel like I say that continuously, but you have no idea what all of y'all have done for me and my kids since I first met you."

He runs his finger across my cheek. Such a simple touch, yet I'm filled with want and need. "See you tomorrow," he promises before turning and heading out of the restaurant.

CHAPTER 4

Matt

"I've got you, Fergie," Jackal yells. I can hear the sounds of gunfire all around me as I'm pulled away from where the RPG exploded. "I've got you." I see him covered in blood, so much damn blood, but my head is pounding, and my skin feels like it's on fire.

The heavy weight on top of me and the soft, insistent whines slowly bring me out of my nightmare. Raising my hand, I feel the soft fur of Champ and release the breath I was unaware I was holding. "Sorry, boy, this is my life," I rumble out. Already, I can feel my heart rate decelerating as the last vestiges of the nightmare fade. As my breathing goes back to normal, Champ moves from being on top of me to right next to me, his tail wagging in a soft, continuous motion. "Good boy, Champ, good boy," I praise. He nuzzles closer and I feel his tongue swipe my cheek. "Not sure that's appropriate, but I'll take it. C'mon, since we're both awake, how about I take you outside?" He jumps off the bed and I swing my legs over, grimacing a bit as the scar tissue pulls. I quickly take a piss then slide a pair of my sweats on in case anyone else is roaming around in the middle of the night. No sense in scaring them shitless seeing my leg.

We quietly make our way through the clubhouse and out the back door where he immediately races off to the area I showed him when I first brought him home. As I look out over what we've created, I start to think about getting my own place. It's time, especially if things with Mandie progress into something more serious. Once Champ has done his business, he leads me back inside and I start to chuckle because he sits in front of the jar that mysteriously appeared on the counter. I open the lid and pull out a treat, then give it to him. He wags his tail and starts heading back to my room while I make a stop at the bar and snag a bottle of beer.

Once again in my room, I decide to catch an episode or two of a show I've been watching until I get tired enough again to attempt sleep. I'm surprised I was able to get five hours in before the nightmare woke me up.

My phone alarm ringing wakes me up. I pick it up and see that somehow, miraculously, I slept for another five hours. With nearly a full night's sleep for a change, I feel energized, so I get up, take a shower and shave, then get dressed before I head down for breakfast.

"Damn, brother, you look almost chipper," Reese states as I stroll into the kitchen, Champ at my side. I walk over and pick up his bowl before I fix his breakfast. Once he's squared away, I pour myself a cup of coffee and sit down across from Reese and Porter.

"Thinking I should've gotten a dog a lot sooner," I admit. "I woke up from a nightmare, nothing unusual about that, and swear to Christ, where normally I would've been up the rest of the night, within thirty minutes or so, I fell back to sleep. Best night's sleep I've gotten in a helluva long time."

"I'm glad to hear it, Matt," Reese replies. I can see the sincerity in his eyes and give him a chin lift in return. When Reese and Porter got out of the military, they formed the Black Tuxedos. Each man who I call brother has served in one capacity or another; most of us under

Reese at some point. While he's devoted to his wife and kids, he still carries a lot of weight on his shoulders worrying about the rest of us.

"You and me both. What has y'all here this morning?" I question.

"Corrie and Kirsten decided to make breakfast for everyone," he says, grinning.

I glance around the kitchen but don't see either woman. At my puzzled look, he starts to laugh so I ask, "And where are these mystery cooks? Did they finally get themselves cloaks of invisibility?"

"Naw, Corrie said we didn't have the ingredients for what they wanted to make, so Garrison took them to the store."

"That makes sense," I murmur.

"You got plans today? We were thinking of doing a cookout later this afternoon," he asks. "Since the girls were hitting up the store, we added to their list so there'll be more than enough."

"Told Mandie that I was going to come over and fix her deck. The damn thing is barely standing."

"So, when you're done, bring her and her kids around. Let her see how we are around here."

I think about his words; if I want to pursue her and see where this attraction goes, she's gonna have to get used to my world. What better way than to come to a family cookout? "Sounds like a plan. I'll ask her when I get there and text you."

"That works for me. Need more?" he questions, pointing to my coffee cup.

I glance at my now-empty cup and nod. "Yeah, brother. Thanks."

Before long, Corrie, Kirsten and the prospect are back, and the kitchen starts to smell like cinnamon and bacon. "We'll have French toast, eggs, and bacon soon," Corrie states. "Oh, and orange juice. No clue why, but Kirsten is craving ice-cold orange juice." I give Porter a look and grin when I see him staring at his old lady.

"Kirsten? You got something you need to tell me?" Porter questions, his eyes roaming up and down her body. Corrie grins as if she knows what's going on as her hand rests on her small baby bump.

"I don't think so, why?" she retorts, sipping on her glass that, sure enough, is filled to the rim with ice and orange juice.

He pointedly looks at her and she shrugs. "Don't you remember how Corrie had cravings with JJ?" he asks. "I think it was frozen lemonades from Chic-fil-A?"

I start chuckling when Kirsten's eyes go wide. "Holy shit, Porter! Do you think? I mean, we haven't exactly done anything to prevent having a baby, but," she stammers, completely at a loss for words. I feel a pang of longing hit me when Porter gets up and crosses the room to pull her into his arms. I don't know what he says, but her face lights up and I watch as he wipes a lone tear that rolls down her cheek.

I want that.

I want that intimacy with someone.

No, strike that.

I want that with *Mandie*.

Mandie

I'm a nervous wreck as I flutter around my house, picking up and straightening before Matt arrives. *Get a grip, girl, he's planning to work outside, not see the inside of your house!* I can't help it though; the lessons I learned from Mama T mean that my house needs to be spotless whenever company comes over, even if they will be outside. I hear Aria cough and cringe. This time of the year is so hard on her with her asthma. It's one of the reasons I quit smoking several years ago. Well, that and it was too expensive, and I'd rather be able to feed my babies than waste money burning cigarettes.

"You feel okay, sweetie?" I ask as I make my way to her.

"Hurts, Mommy," she replies, pointing to her chest. I pick her up, uncaring that she's capable of walking, and head into the bathroom. Once in there, I start the shower, hoping a steam session will help. I'm out of the medicine for her nebulizer; otherwise, I'd give her a breathing treatment.

"Wait right here, Aria," I instruct, pointing to the rug in front of the bathtub. "Mommy needs to get something." I rush into my room and grab the pulse oximeter that one nurse gave me the last time we went so I could keep an eye on things at home. Once I'm back in the bathroom, I slip it on her finger and watch the numbers. As long as she's over eighty-five, we should be okay and not have to run to the hospital. Seeing that it's ninety-two makes my heart slow back to normal. "Okay, we're going to sit in here for a little bit and see if that helps."

"I don't like dis, Mommy."

"I know, sweetie. I'm sorry." I guess I need to call her doctor and see if she'll call in some albuterol for the nebulizer. Thank God I have money tucked back now, although with both kids on Medicaid, most of the time their prescriptions are pretty cheap. Still, I remember quite a few times when I turned in aluminum cans to get enough money to cover that and those memories are what fuel me, on the days I'm exhausted, to keep on going so I can make a better life for all of us.

Twenty minutes later, I have her changed and lying on the couch watching her favorite show while I get Beau up and changed. When a knock comes on the door, I put him on a blanket in front of the couch with some toys and go answer it. "Hey, Matt," I say as I open the door wider.

"Hope I'm not too early," he replies.

"Not at all. I was just getting the kids settled in." He glances at the two kids and I see a look of concern cross his face.

"Is she okay?" he asks, pointing to Aria.

"Her asthma is flaring up."

"Do you need to take her to get checked? I can drive if you want me to."

"I think we're okay right now. Just did a steam session."

"Does she have medicine to take?"

"She's out of the stuff for her nebulizer right now. I have to call her doctor on Monday."

"Are they not open today?" he questions.

I glance at the clock hanging on the living room wall. "I can try to call, but they don't work on Sundays. Regardless, they have an after-hours number and her history is well-known, so it's worth a shot to call. Do you need anything from me to get started?"

"Not at all, just wanted to let you know I was here."

I smile up at him, grateful that his protective nature has him wanting to do this for me. "Let me know if you do; I made some tea and also have lemonade."

"I'll probably hit you up for some of that in a little while," he states.

I watch him go back down the stairs and over to his truck. He starts pulling stuff out and I notice a dog lying by the tree I have in my front yard. "Is he yours?" I ask, standing in the doorway.

"Yeah, just got him a few days ago. His name is Champ; he's a service dog. Supposed to help me with my PTSD." My heart breaks for him. I think I likely have it to some extent after what Alistair did, but I'm sure it's nothing compared to what he endured being in the military. Not that he's told me he served, but I've seen the dog tags underneath his T-shirt a few times and I'd be remiss if I hadn't noticed his awesome tattoo. It's just like the others that the men in the Black Tuxedos sport, so that tells me that they likely served at the same time, or close enough.

I hear Aria cough and turn to tend to my daughter. Grabbing my phone, I say a silent prayer of thanks that Matt's generosity has given me the minutes I need to make the call to her doctor. Once I reach a nurse and explain the situation, she advises that she'll call in an inhaler as well as more medicine for her nebulizer. I breathe a sigh of relief; she can go downhill so quickly that it's scary.

"Mommy is going to call Olive to see if she'll go and pick up your medicine, okay, sweetie?" I ask.

"Okay, Mommy." She looks sleepy so I cover her with the quilt that's on the back of the couch, then call Olive, who promises to go and get the prescriptions when they're ready and bring them by. With that all sorted, I head into the kitchen to start working on lunch. Since Matt is fixing my deck, I plan to feed him as well. It's the least I can do. I decide on barbecue sandwiches, since I made a roast in the crockpot the other night. Pulling out the container of leftovers, I shred the meat then add barbecue sauce before putting it in a pan and turning the stove on low to simmer in the sauce. Thanks to the generosity of a stranger, I have options at my fingertips, so I pull out some potatoes and quickly peel them then get them cut up for homemade fries.

Once everything is ready, I make a plate for Matt, pour a glass of tea and carefully carry it to the front door. When I get the door opened, I'm blown away at how much he's managed to accomplish in such a short time. "This looks awesome," I declare, looking around. He has expanded my deck and is currently working on covering it which means I won't get soaked anymore when it rains and I'm trying to get the kids inside.

"Thanks," he replies. I hand him the plate with the sandwiches and fries, as well as his tea and a bottle of ketchup. "What's this?"

"Thought you might be hungry, so I made you barbecue sandwiches and some fries," I say.

"If they taste half as good as they smell, I'm in for a treat," he states, grinning at me.

"Well, Aria is wearing a lot of hers but she's little so probably not a good judge." His chuckles have me smiling.

"Were you able to reach the doctor?"

"Yeah I was and they called in the stuff for her nebulizer, as well as an inhaler. Olive is going to pick it up for me and bring it out."

"That's good. If you think she's feeling up to it, we're having a cookout later at the clubhouse. I'd like to take you and the kids." I think about his offer. I'd like to get to know everyone outside of when I see them at work.

"She should be, but I can always drive separately just in case."

"I've got you, Mandie. If she starts feeling bad, I'll bring y'all back home."

"Thank you, Matt. I'll uh let you get back to work. Do I need to bring anything for the cookout?"

"Just you and the kids. Corrie and Kirsten bought out the store and I'm sure that they'll have everything sorted."

I nod even though I'll go inside and make something for dessert. Mama T taught me to always bring something whenever I was invited to someone's house. I know I can put together a cake or some cookies at least. "Let me know if you want more tea. In fact, just feel free to come inside and grab it since I might be tied up with the kids."

"Will do."

When Olive arrives, I get Aria set up with a breathing treatment which seems to help her further. She still looks a bit peaked, but I think as long as she takes it easy, we should be able to go with Matt to the cookout with his club. I'm looking forward to being around other adults. I know I work in a restaurant, but those interactions are superficial at best. I need more adult friends; Olive is great, but she's still only a teenager and has no real understanding about what being an adult with responsibilities is all about.

"So, you're going to their clubhouse?" Olive questions as she helps me make cookies. They're the recipe that Mama T taught me years ago; double chocolate chunk, and surprisingly, I had all the ingredients.

"Yeah. Ollie, he told me last night at work that he's interested in me," I whisper so he doesn't hear me. Granted, he's outside and the door and windows are all closed, but I'm not taking any chances.

"Why wouldn't he be? You're freaking awesome, Mandie," she declares.

"Because I'm a single mom with two kids. That kind of stuff just doesn't happen," I insist.

"Why the hell not? You deserve to be happy just as much as the next person, girl. Now, what else do you need to do to get ready?"

I glance down at myself and grimace. I'm a sweaty, hot mess thanks to the cleaning I did earlier and Aria's sweat session in the bathroom. "I need a shower," I admit.

"Then go grab one. I'll keep an eye on the kids."

"Ollie, it's your off day," I protest.

"So? Can't a friend help another friend out from time to time?" she retorts. "You're only a few years older than me, Mandie, and you're my best friend. I know I don't know all the ways of the world, but that's okay. I can watch and learn."

"Fine, fine. I'll go shower and get myself ready. I have no clue what to wear though."

"Thinking jeans and a shirt will work." Her sassy reply has me grinning back because I've got plenty of both.

CHAPTER 5

Matt

"Let me tell her I'm running to get cleaned up and will be back, Champ," I tell the dog as I put the rest of my tools away. The only thing left is to get the deck stained and weather-protected with some polyurethane, but it's supposed to rain for the next few days, so it'll have to wait. He woofs at me before jumping into the truck to hang his head out the window.

I walk back up the stairs and knock, my eyes roaming her yard to see if there's anything I forgot. "Hey, Matt. Oh! You're finished!" Her voice is almost breathless as she speaks and I temporarily forget why I knocked to begin with, such is her effect on me.

"Other than getting it stained and protected from the weather, but it's gonna rain, so that has to wait. I'll be back in about thirty minutes or so, just need to grab a shower and get cleaned up. Just wanted to give you a heads-up."

"We'll be ready when you get back," she promises.

Without thinking, I run my index finger down her cheek. Her skin is so fucking soft it's maddening. When I feel the unmistakable tightening of my cock behind my jeans, I want to throw my fist in the air. Since she came into my life, I've had twinges, of course, but knowing that she's the cause tells me that the fucking psychologist was correct. For whatever reason, Jessa's bitchiness caused me to have my issue. "I'll see y'all shortly," I reply before turning around to head back to my truck. It won't do for her to see what she does to me, at least not yet.

It took less time than I expected to get to the clubhouse, showered, changed and be on my way back to her place. When I arrive, I walk over to her car and get the two car seats from the back and install them in my truck, making a mental note to buy some so that we don't have to switch them out constantly. Her car is fine, but it's too small for a man of my size. Once I'm sure that the seats are secure, I head up the stairs and knock. Her flushed face greets me, and I memorize each small detail; the deep blue of her eyes, the length of her lashes, the tiny freckles that cross her nose. "Hey, sweetheart, y'all ready?"

"Yes, I just need to grab Beau's diaper bag and the cookies. Aria? Come on, sweetie," she calls out. I hear tiny feet running down the hall and watch as Aria skids to a stop in front of me.

"I'm weady, Mr. Matt," she exclaims. She's holding a doll that's almost half her size and a small purse is slung over her shoulder. I don't think I've ever seen anything cuter in my damn life.

"Let's get your brother then so your mom can get the cookies, okay?" I ask.

"Him's over there," she states, pointing to the swing that's in the corner. I walk over to the swing and bring it to a stop and watch in amazement as his gaze shifts to me. Instead of hollering, he raises his arms up so I pick him up and settle him against me.

"He's kinda heavy," I say, causing Mandie to giggle.

"He's my chunky monkey, aren't you, pumpkin?" she coos. Beau babbles at his mother and I chuckle at the normalcy of the situation. "Okay, I think I have everything."

"Then let's get this party started," I decree, following her out the door once I've made sure it's locked behind me. I manage to make it to the passenger side door and get it open before she reaches it, then shift Beau so that I can give her a hand up.

"Up, pwease," Aria instructs.

"Give him a minute, pumpkin, and let him get Beau settled," Mandie states.

I grin at the tone she uses because the little girl's face falls and she starts to pout. "You think you can help me get him in?" I ask her, leaning down.

"I can twy!" she asserts. Chuckling, I open the back door and with one arm, get her into her seat before I go to the other side and get Beau strapped in. I double-check Aria's buckles, not surprised that she has done it herself. She seems relatively independent and something inside breaks that this little girl has had to learn that at such a young age. Not that I fault Mandie; far from it. I know she's doing the best she can with the hand she's been dealt. Only, she has a new dealer in town now.

Me.

Mandie

I wasn't sure what to expect when we got to the club-house, but the feeling of family and camaraderie surrounds us as two little ones run around giggling and blowing bubbles. "Hey, Mandie!" Corrie calls out. "Come sit with us. Oh, aren't you cute?" she states to Aria. "Shayla, I think she's close to Meli's age."

"How old is she?" Shayla inquires.

"She'll be four soon," I reply. "She's tiny for her age, though." The guilt that swamps me at that fact has my head dropping.

"Nothing wrong with being petite, Mandie," Matt rumbles out, setting Beau down in a playpen that I didn't even notice was set up.

"Aria, here are some bubbles," Shayla says to my daughter. I'm listening to all the conversations and the longing that wells up inside takes me by surprise.

This is a family.

They may not be biologically related, but they're family, nonetheless.

I want that for my kids. I want the fun, the extra aunts and uncles, the love.

Beau, meanwhile, has grabbed a truck and is banging it on the bottom of the playpen, gurgling and babbling. I watch as Shayla shows Aria how to blow bubbles and smile through the tears.

"You okay, sweetheart?" Matt whispers.

"Yeah." I don't really know what to say. I mean, we're just starting out and hell, up until he said that to me last night, I never in my wildest dreams thought it was a possibility.

"I'm gonna go grab a drink, what would you like?"

"Lemonade?" I ask. At my response, the women start laughing.

"You're not the butt of a joke," Corrie says, seeing the look on my face. "It's just that when I was pregnant, I craved frozen lemonades and apparently, Kirsten here, is craving ice-cold orange juice. It just struck us as funny." And in my case, it would be a miracle seeing as I haven't had sex in almost two years, give or take. Beau is nearly a year old now, and Alistair left when I found out about the pregnancy.

"Oh, congratulations," I reply, looking at Kirsten. Then, staring closer at Corrie, I see her small baby bump. "And I guess for you as well."

"May as well make it a trifecta," Shayla states, pointing down at her stomach. She's barely showing but I can see the glow surrounding her.

"All three of you?" I whisper.

Their laughter rings out again as they nod at me. "Our poor men already don't know what to do with us half the time," Corrie snickers out between giggles. "Add in the fact that the three of us have pregnancy hormones and I suspect they'll all be bald soon."

"We're gonna need you to be the voice of reason, Mandie," Shayla intones. She tries so hard to look serious but loses it when I start giggling.

"If I'm the voice of reason, we're all screwed, y'all," I advise. That sets them off again and I watch as the three of them nearly collapse into each other, laughing so hard that they're crying.

"Good to see you making new friends," Matt teases as he returns with my lemonade. I turn to look up at him and see him grinning down at me. He's so damn good-looking that it still blows me away that he wants me.

"I think they've lost their marbles," I whisper. "Did you know all three of them are *pregnant?*"

"So Shayla finally figured it out as well," he murmurs.

"Does everyone live here?" I question, figuring that's likely how they know so much about one another.

"Just us single guys, although sometimes, if we're here late, the others will stay in their rooms they have here." I nod, even though I don't fully understand. "But we're a close-knit group, so we spend a lot of time with each other."

While I watch, the other men come over and scoop up their women, sit down, then place them back on their laps. Not missing a beat, Matt pulls up a chair, plops his ass down then pulls me so I'm sitting across his lap, my legs dangling off to one side. I can feel the heat from his leather vest that he put on once we got to the clubhouse seeping into my shirt. The smell surrounds me; leather, oil, and something faintly woodsy, that I know has become my favorite scent in the world.

"Rex! How long before the meat is done?" Reese calls out.

"It's done when it's done and not a minute sooner, as-um, butthead," Rex replies, looking at the kids watching him.

"Good save, Rex," Corrie yells, causing all of us to laugh.

Before long, Rex hollers out that the meats are done, and I stand with the other women as we prepare the kids' plates. Beau is still mostly on baby food, but I've been introducing some softer foods to his diet, so I make a plate for him as well. "You go get them situated and I'll fix you a plate," Matt says. "Anything you don't like?"

"No, not really. I mean, I won't eat any kind of exotic meat like gator or snake, but it looks like y'all made regular old hamburgers and hot dogs," I reply.

He tucks a loose strand of hair behind my ear before he leans in and says, "Yeah, I won't eat that either. Do you want a burger or a dog?"

"Burger, please." My response comes out breathless and I chalk it up to the fact he's so close. Granted, I've been sitting on his lap for some time now, but still, the impact he has on me is mind-blowing.

"Be back in a few," he advises as he gently pushes me toward where Aria is now sitting, chattering away with her new little friends. I set her plate down and quickly cut her hot dog into manageable pieces before I hand her a fork.

"Looks good, Mommy," she says. I'm fortunate that she's not a picky eater. Judging from the little boy's plate, as well as the other little girl's, they aren't either. I kiss her head and pat her back before I take the other plate I fixed for Beau and move toward the table near the playpen.

Picking him up, I grin. He's such a happy baby and when he sees the food, he starts banging his hand against my shoulder. "Shush, Beau," I say. "Mommy will get you fed in just a minute. Patience is a virtue."

"Not for a little boy," Reese quips, walking over with a highchair in tow. "Thought this might make it easier for you to feed him."

"God, yes. He's quite messy." I glance down at my shirt, which now bears a slobbery handprint, causing Reese to laugh.

"Nothing a little water won't fix," he advises.

"Or in Beau's case, a lot of water," I reply, remembering the dirt from a few days ago. I get my baby boy situated and let him go to town with the finger foods I got for him, keeping a close eye so he doesn't decide to overstuff his mouth.

Matt returns with two plates laden down with food and I feel my brows raise. There's no freaking way I can eat all of that! He sees my look and says, "Whatever you can't eat, I'll finish." Once he's set our plates down, he goes back to the coolers and returns with fresh drinks for both of us.

As the afternoon progresses, the men pull out cornhole boards and soon, we're embroiled in a guys against girls game while the kids play in the playground area. I'm thrilled to see Aria and Amelia playing together and have to hold my laughter back when I notice that Reese and Corrie's little boy, JJ, is acting like one of the guys. He's standing back, his little arms across his chest while the girls giggle with their dolls. "They're so stinking cute," Corrie whispers. I turn to say something and notice she's crying.

"Why are you crying?" I murmur back, hoping to keep her man from noticing.

She waves her hand in front of her face. "Pregnancy hormones. I'm either crying, eating, sleeping or fu- um, you know," she replies, her face turning red. I start laughing because I know where she was going with her response. I remember those hormones and even though I was single during my pregnancy with Beau, I was a hot mess most nights.

"For fuck's sake, Corrie, what has you weepy now?" Reese asks, a smirk on his face. Obviously, this isn't unusual for her, because he pulls her into his chest, and I hear her contented sigh.

"Just watching the kids while we wait for our turn," she says. He glances over to where the three older kids are playing and starts chuckling.

"I think we're witnessing a future prospect, brothers," he calls out, nodding his head to JJ.

"Train 'em young," Nick advises.

"He's learning from some of the best men I know," Matt states, coming to stand next to me. Leaning in, he asks, "Do we need to get the kids home? I know it's getting late."

I glance at my phone and see what time it is and reluctantly say, "Yeah, I have a class tomorrow and then I have to work for a few hours. Plus, they both need baths."

"Alright, let's get them rounded up," he replies.

I touch his arm to stop him and murmur, "I've had a good time today, Matt. Thank you for bringing us."

"My pleasure, sweetheart," he returns, leaning in and kissing my forehead. Such a simple act yet it warms me to my soul. How is it possible to be falling for someone based on a few minimal touches?

CHAPTER 6

Mandie

LAST NIGHT AFTER MATT BROUGHT US HOME, HE helped me get both kids inside before leaving. As we stood at the door, he reached over and pulled me into a hug. That simple embrace stayed with me all night, through several breathing treatments for Aria, and one midnight bath after a coughing spell made her throw up. As I stand under the beating shower, I roll my head on my shoulders in an attempt to ease the tension that has me strung tight. Hearing Aria cry out, I fly out of the shower, pulling my robe on over my wet body.

"I'm here, sweetie," I croon as I pull her close. Noticing that her lips are blue-tinged, I decide that we need medical intervention because what I've been doing isn't working. "Let me call Olive and have her come to watch Beau." Aria lays in my arms, limp and wheezing.

My fear ramps up as I carry her in my arms back to my room, where my phone sits on the nightstand. Grabbing it, I quickly call Ollie and she tells me she'll be there in a few minutes and to call for an ambulance.

I can't afford an ambulance, but right now, my sweet girl is struggling. I'll figure out a way to pay it later. I place her on my bed and prop her up with pillows to hopefully ease her breathing and get dressed as fast as possible, while talking to the dispatcher. She advises that an ambulance is being dispatched and I send up a prayer that Ollie arrives before they do so that Beau is taken care of. With nothing to do but wait, I move us to the living room and grab her inhaler. She hates using it, but I need her to get more air into her little lungs, so I hold her as I squeeze the inhaler. She coughs and wheezes a little bit after the second puff, then bursts into tears.

"Hurts, Mommy," she wails.

"I know, sweetie, I know." I hear the knock on my door before Ollie walks in and despite the circumstances, I smile. She must have literally walked out the door when I called because she's wearing a SpongeBob onesie and her hair is sticking up everywhere.

"How is she?" she immediately asks, coming over to the couch.

"Not good," I whisper. I can feel the fear trying to paralyze me, but I push it back. I need to keep calm so that Aria does. "Can you maybe pack a few things for us really quick? I don't know what'll happen, but I suspect we'll be admitted." She nods and rushes down the hall to gather up some clothes and Aria's favorite doll. I don't think to ask for any of my hygiene items; it's not on my radar right now.

I hear the siren and breathe a sigh of relief. "Help is here, Aria," I croon. She's almost lifeless at this point and terror takes hold of me. The paramedics rush into my house and immediately take her from my arms, leaving me feeling bereft.

"Ma'am, we need to take her to the hospital," the older woman advises as they strap my little girl onto the gurney. They've already got an oxygen mask on her and an IV started.

"Yes, of course," I reply, grabbing my purse and the bag that Olive shoves into my arms. "I'll call you when I know something. Kiss Beau for me, please."

"I've got you, Mandie," she replies.

With nothing to do but sit by my little girl's side as they work on her, I send up a silent prayer that she'll be okay.

I can't lose her; she and Beau are the most important things in my life.

"We're going to admit her," the emergency room doctor advises. They've done a blood gas test and I'm still holding back the tears at how my daughter screamed while in restraints. Right now, they've given her something to calm her down, as well as some heavy-duty steroids and an antibiotic. "She's in respiratory distress, Miss Matchum. I'm glad you called for help."

"She started yesterday and had four breathing treatments, as well as one use of her inhaler before I called. Should I have called sooner?" I question.

"Unfortunately, with asthma, a child can go downhill quickly. It sounds like you were following the protocol her doctor has you on."

"Yes, sir. I didn't check her numbers today because her lips were turning blue, so I knew she needed help."

"She's going to be fine, Miss Matchum. We're getting the admission paperwork done now and will get her settled into a room. I presume you'll be staying with her."

"Absolutely." I know Beau is in good hands and that if she needs to, Olive will take him home with her so that Maria can help.

It takes another hour before we're finally in a room. I look at Aria, so small and still, in a pediatric hospital gown. She's got an oxygen mask on and while I don't understand all the medical jargon, I know they've got it set at one hundred percent. Her left arm is strapped to a board and there's an IV that is connected to three different bags of medicine. The worst part is that because she's getting so much fluid-wise, they've put her in a pull-up, something she hates. As I sink into the recliner next to her, my mind races.

I forgot to notify my instructor. Most of my classes are now online, but I had a video conference this morning that I missed. Pulling out my phone, I send her an email to apologize and let her know what is going on. Then, I call The Steakhouse. When Juan answers, I say, "I can't come in, Juan, and I don't know when I'll be able to this week. Aria's in the hospital."

"We know, sweetheart. Don't worry about a thing. You have sick time and I'll put that in for you." At his words, tears begin to stream down my face. I'm not full-time per se, but Juan and Maria set it up so that as long as an employee works at least thirty hours a week, they earn time off. I never use mine because I have no clue when one of the kids will get sick and knowing that I have time that's banked eases a bit of my burden.

"Thank you. And thank Ollie and Maria too because I'm sure Beau will be at your house while we're up here."

"He's already there and Nonna Maria is in hog heaven," he states, laughing.

"So he'll come home more spoiled than he already is," I surmise.

"Most likely. Now, what do you and the little princess need?"

"Not sure. Ollie packed a bag for me but honestly, I haven't looked to see what's in it."

"I'll bring you some food later. Hospital food sucks."

"You don't have to do that, Juan."

"Yes, I do. Y'all are family and that's what family does. I'll see you two later. Kiss that baby for us," he instructs.

"Thank you, I will. See you later." I disconnect the call and sit there, my mind whirling and spinning until I finally fall into a light doze, my hand clutching Aria's in a tight grip.

Matt

I smile on my way to The Steakhouse. They have several lunch specials and the need to see Mandie over-rides everything else. I wanted so badly to kiss her last night before I left but was afraid it was too soon.

You're a monster, you repulse me. Jessa's words come to the forefront of my mind and I shove them back. I know now that the woman I dated in high school, the one I thought was my forever, was shallow and narrow-minded. While I'm still nervous as fuck about Mandie seeing all the scars, instinctively I know that for her, it won't matter.

Despite everything she's been through, she has an innate goodness that runs through her. I don't know her whole history, but it'll happen and I'm content to let it play out for the time being. I pull into the restaurant's parking lot and frown when I don't see her car. I know she mentioned she works most days, at least during lunch, so she should be here right now.

I get out of my truck and head inside after putting my cut on. Seeing Juan, I walk over and ask, "Where is Mandie?"

"She's at the hospital," he replies, a sad look on his face.

"Is she okay? Did she have an accident?" I fire question after question at him until he raises his hand for me to stop.

"It's Aria, she apparently had an asthma attack that was severe enough to put her into respiratory distress. They've admitted her for a few days at least, so they can get things turned around. She apparently had an underlying case of pneumonia that triggered everything."

"Does she need anything?" Right now, all I want is to be by her side, but first, I have to make sure she has what she needs to take care of herself and that sweet girl. "What about Beau?" I know she doesn't have any family, so what will she do with him?

"My wife and daughter have him at our house. It's not our first rodeo with Little Miss, unfortunately. I plan to take her some food tonight, but if you're going up there, let me put something together for her for now. Knowing Mandie, she hasn't eaten."

I nod then ask, "If it's not too much trouble, can I place an order for myself?"

"I already planned to make yours as well," Juan advises. "Go, sit at the bar and have a soda or something. I'll have it out to you shortly." I walk over to the bar and ask for a Sprite, which the bartender quickly places in front of me with a wink.

In a short amount of time, although it feels like hours, I'm back in my truck, the smells from the bag causing my stomach to rumble as I head toward the hospital. I already notified Reese, who advised me to find out what Mandie needed so the club could help. He also let me know that they'd take care of Champ for me, at least until I get back to the clubhouse. An idea starts circulating in my mind and I hope she'll at least listen to what I have to say.

Walking into the hospital, I'm hit with the smells that take me back to my own stay. I know hospitals are a necessary evil and of course, a lot of good things happen like babies and shit, but right now, there's a little girl struggling to breathe and a mom who is likely at the end of her proverbial rope, so I push my aversion aside and stride over to the information desk and within seconds am heading to the elevator.

It's time to claim my woman.

That thought no longer scares me. I know we have a lot to learn about one another and I sure as hell don't expect anything right now, but I'm hoping in time we'll build something based on mutual respect and friendship.

And if love eventually comes, I'm okay with that too.

I take a deep breath before I walk into the room to prepare myself for whatever I might see. Opening the door as quietly as possible, I feel my heart drop when I glance over and notice that Aria is in a bed, a clear tent-like thing covering her. Mandie is laying with her head near her daughter's, outside the tent, and I can tell she's beyond exhausted. Despite the dark circles under her eyes, she's still the prettiest woman I've ever seen. I place the bag of food onto the rolling table and pick her up from the recliner, sit back down and curl her into my arms.

She never moves, even though in her sleep, she snuggles closer. Placing a soft kiss on her temple, I silently vow that her struggles are a thing of the past.

CHAPTER 7

Mandie

As I slowly wake up, I become aware of strong arms holding me close. When I finally dozed off while watching Aria sleep, I was in a recliner next to her bed. Now, I'm in a pair of muscle-bound arms that I recognize, even in my sleepy haze.

Matt.

Matt is here, only how did he find out? I didn't think to call him, so used to handling things on my own.

"You're thinking too hard, sweetheart," he murmurs. His sleep-roughened voice sends tingles throughout my body.

Get a grip, Mandie! Now's not the time or the place.

"What...how...Matt, how did you find out where I was?" I finally ask.

"Wanted to see you so I went to The Steakhouse for lunch. Juan told me," he replies. I feel him shift beneath me, then the lightest touch, as soft as what I imagine butterfly wings would feel like brushes against the top of my head. Call me a hopeless romantic, but I've always wanted a man who would do those little things; kiss my forehead, brush back my hair, hold me when I cry.

"Beau! I need to check on him," I cry out as I pull away.

He tightens his arms and says, "He's fine. Juan said that Olive took him over to their house. They've got him; your only focus right now is on Aria, okay?"

I nod as tears begin to streak down my face. "I should've known, Matt," I whisper, looking at my daughter. She looks so small in the hospital bed. They decided at some point to put the oxygen tent around her and I say a silent prayer that it's working. My eyes glance at the monitor over her bed and a ghost of a smile crosses my lips. "It's working," I murmur.

"What's working?" he asks.

"They decided to add the oxygen tent because even with the oxygen at full strength, her numbers were crappy. Look, though, they're coming up!" I state, pointing.

"It's at ninety," he announces. "Shouldn't it be higher?"

I turn and look at him. "When she got here, her numbers were in the high fifties, Matt. She was in respiratory distress. I could've lost her!" I feel the moment that I lose it, because he pulls me close as sobs wrack my body. I should have seen she was struggling, but I was so thrilled that she was playing and had made some new friends, I didn't even notice.

He doesn't say anything, he just runs his hands up and down my back. His touch is soothing, and I find myself relaxing in his embrace while all the fear and terror of the past hours wash out of me. As I sit back a bit and start wiping my face from the tears, his hand comes up and he swipes them away with his thumb. "You're not alone in this, Mandie," he states. "I've got you now."

His touch is gentle and calming, despite his size. I'm not sure what I've done right in this life to warrant having a man like him show interest, but I'm going to grab the brass ring with both hands. I may be scared shitless about any kind of physical relationship, but maybe he'll give me the time I need to wrap my mind around exposing myself like that to another man. Alistair was less than complimentary, and his words sometimes play on a loop in my head.

You're kind of chunky now, Mandie. Your hips spread after the baby. Those stretch marks are disgusting. Breastfeeding has made your tits sag.

"You're in your head again, Mandie. Do you want to share?" he asks.

Sighing, I look up at him, only to see the warmth in his gaze. There's no judgment and that loosens my memories. "My ex wasn't very nice, Matt."

Steel bands tighten around me as he states, "Explain that."

"We were both foster care kids and became friends at my last house. Mama T was something, Matt. She treated us like we were her own flesh and blood. That's where I learned how to cook and keep a house. Anyway, we turned eighteen and decided we'd live together. I got pregnant with Aria, which he wasn't too thrilled about, but after growing up with parents who loved me, then having Mama T when they passed away, I wanted someone to love, you know?" He nods and I take a deep breath before continuing. "He wasn't very reliable with working. He'd find a job, work for a few weeks, maybe a month, then he'd quit or get fired because he'd get pissed off. So, I did what I could to help keep a roof over our heads and make sure that Aria had what she needed."

As the memories flood over me, I feel tears slipping down my face, which he wipes away.

"You can stop if you need to, baby," he murmurs.

"No, I'm good," I reply. "Anyway, the day I found out I was pregnant with Beau, I told him, figuring that would make him straighten up, you know? Only...only it didn't."

"What did he do?" His voice is low and menacing and if it weren't for the gentle hands still running up and down my back and arms, I'd be worried.

"He, uh, he didn't take the news well," I whisper. That's an understatement if ever I heard one.

"How so?" Now, his tone is even lower, causing me to shiver. "Sorry, sweetheart, but I get the impression that he hurt you."

"He did." My voice is so small, I don't think he hears me until I feel his arms pull me even closer.

"Never again, sweetheart. You hear me?" His vehement response has me relaxing.

I'm so lost in the memories that I continue talking, taking comfort in his embrace. "He beat me that day, pretty badly in fact, then took off. I came to and managed to get to Aria. It took me a few weeks to recover, Matt." The police had wanted me to file charges, so I did, but it made no difference. Alistair was gone and based on his last actions, he was never coming back, a fact I wasn't too torn up about, all things considered.

"Fuck, Mandie. He put his hands on you?" I hear the rage in his voice and feel his arms tighten around me at my words and know instinctively that this man would cut off his arm before he'd ever hurt a woman.

"Yeah. It wasn't the first time, but he'd never gone that far before," I admit, shame lacing my tone. I never thought I'd let that happen to me, yet it did and the mortification I still feel has my face heating. "I was making plans to leave when I found out about Beau." The bastard had stolen the majority of the money I had hidden away, but he didn't get it all which was a good thing since it kept me afloat until I was able to work.

"Has he been back?" I shake my head violently at his question.

"No. I think...I think he left town completely. The police weren't able to find him. I've got a protective order, though, in case he ever decides to come back. Plus, because of his actions, I was able to get his rights terminated." I once again count my lucky stars that Juan and Maria entered my life because they helped me get all of that accomplished. It may be scary sometimes being the one that the kids are wholly dependent on, but I know I'll do anything for them.

"So you've been doing all of this on your own?"

"With the help of Juan, Maria and Olive," I reply.

"So fucking strong," he whispers, kissing my temple.

"Not really, Matt. I just didn't have anything to fall back on, so I had to keep moving forward. I'm just lucky that Juan hired me when he did." I giggle, remembering that day. Who the hell goes into a prospective interview pregnant with a toddler on their hip?

"You've got me too now, sweetheart," he advises. "And with me, comes the club."

I'm about to reply when I hear Aria whimpering. I jump up from his lap and reach over to touch her through the holes in the tent. "Shhh, Mommy's here, pumpkin."

"Hurts, Mommy," Aria cries, rubbing her chest.

"I know, I know. Your lungs are sick, sweetie. You're getting medicine to make them all better, okay?" Her plaintive cries are breaking my heart and I feel tears sliding down my face once again. At this rate, I'll be dehydrated.

"Let me go get the nurse," Matt says, standing and heading toward the door.

I send him a grateful smile then focus back on my daughter. "Let's sit you up a little bit, okay?" I ask, pushing the button on the side of the bed to raise it a little. "That might help."

"Look who's awake," the nurse says as she comes into the room. I like the pediatric wing here; all the nurses wear cartoon scrubs and genuinely care for the little ones. "Let me check you over, Miss Aria," she says, before opening up the oxygen tent. I step back slightly, still holding my sweet girl's hand and watch as the nurse takes her vitals. "She's doing better. I think we can go back to the mask instead of the tent. That way, you can crawl in next to her," she tells me. That's something else I like about this place; I can cuddle my child and help keep her calm which will let her body heal.

"How-how do her lungs sound?"

"A lot clearer. There's still some crackling, but the medicine is working. I'll give the doctor an update and see if he wants another blood gas draw. I'm sure we'll need another X-ray, but that might not be for a day or two."

I cringe when I hear her say they may need another blood gas test, not looking forward to seeing my sweet girl restrained again while she cries in pain. When I glance at Aria, I notice her hair is all matted from the fever. "Can I give her a bath?"

"That shouldn't be a problem. Why don't you get it ready and I'll cap off her IV and put a waterproof covering over it? I'm sure she'll feel better once she's nice and clean." I nod and head into the bathroom, Matt following behind me.

"Do you need me to go get anything? I have food here from Juan, but we probably need to heat it up."

"There's a family area just past the nurse's station with a microwave," I reply as I work to get the water temperature adjusted.

He heads off to take care of reheating our food and I carry my girl into the bathroom, a clean hospital gown and pull-up in my arms as well. "Mommy, I don't want to wear that," Aria states as I undress her.

I set her on the toilet and say, "I know, pumpkin, but with everything they're giving you, I don't want you to have an accident in your panties. How about this, when you're awake, I'll carry you in to use the potty."

"Okay, Mommy. I's a big girl now and don't need them." I grin because Aria is spunky and sassy, but not a brat.

"How about we get you cleaned up?" I ask once she's finished. She grins and lets me take her hospital gown off and place her in the tub.

"This feels good, Mommy," she says. I take my time washing and conditioning her hair while she haphazardly washes her body. Once her hair is squeaky clean again, I take over for her and before long, she's clean, dried, powdered and back in a new hospital gown and pull-up.

"Okay, pumpkin, let's get you back into bed," I state, standing.

"I've got her," Matt says, scaring the shit out of me. I had no idea he had returned, and I can feel my heart racing.

"You scared me half to death," I tell him, my hand over my heart.

"I'm sorry, sweetheart," he replies before scooping up Aria and carrying her back to her bed. I don't know what he says, but she's giggling as he gently puts her in the middle of the bed then covers her up.

I walk over with a brush and towel so that I can dry her hair then get it combed out. "Let Mommy fix your hair, Aria," I say as I crawl into the bed and place her between my legs. "Do you want me to braid it?" I question.

"Yes, pwease, Mommy," she replies, looking back at me. I lean down and kiss her chin, thankful that her lips are back to their normal bubblegum pink color and not tinged with blue. That sight alone took ten years off my life. Matt picks up the remote for the television and starts scrolling through to find something for her to watch while I lose myself in the simple task of drying her hair then braiding it 'like Anna' does. She loves the movie *Frozen* and I make a mental note to call Ollie and see if she'll bring the stuffed Olaf that she sleeps with every night.

"Do you want me to call Ollie and see if she'll bring Olaf and Poppy for you?" She also loves the *Trolls*, especially Poppy. The stuffed one that Juan and Maria got for her is nearly half her size, but she doesn't care. She has tea parties with them several times a week that Beau, Ollie and me attend.

"I can run and get it for you, so Olive doesn't have to go back out with the baby if you'd like," Matt says. "Do you have anything else you want me to grab?"

I stop and think; the trip here was so quick that I brought nothing with me except the bag Ollie gave me and after looking at what she packed, I still need stuff. I'm going to need at least a change or two of clothes, my brush and also my personal hygiene items. I'm a little hesitant to let him see the state of my wardrobe but he's right, Ollie doesn't need to be hauling Beau around or bringing him up to the hospital. I don't want him exposed unnecessarily to the germs this place holds. "You wouldn't mind?" I hesitantly ask.

"Not at all. Write a list, Mandie, and I'll get it taken care of. I'm sure you'd be more comfortable in lounging clothes than jeans." I giggle because he's right. When I'm home, it's sweats, shorts, leggings; my jeans are pretty much reserved for work or when I have to run errands.

I finish Aria's hair then slide out from behind her. Once she's comfortably sitting up, I slide the tray table in front of her and open up a container of applesauce that the nurse brought in earlier. "Here, sweetie, how about a snack?"

"Speaking of snacks, come and eat, Mandie. You need to keep your own strength up." I nod and walk over to the recliner, plopping my ass down on the seat, which is surprisingly comfortable. When I see what Juan sent, I grin.

"Aria, I think Papa Juan was thinking of you too, sweetie," I state as I lean over and put a small container on her tray. "Look what he made for you."

"Mouse tails and red sauce, my faborite!" she exclaims, causing both of us to laugh.

Matt leans in and whispers, "Mouse tails?"

I can't help it; I start laughing harder. "She watched some animated movie that had cute mice in it. Anyhow, the first time she got a plate of spaghetti, she proclaimed they were mouse tails and that's what she's called them ever since."

"She's fucking adorable, Mandie. You've done a good job," he says before digging into what I know is one of the best steak sandwiches in Texas. Of course, everything that comes out of Juan's kitchen is superb. I give him a small smile; most of the time I feel like I'm barely treading water, yet he walked in this morning and has told me I'm strong and that I'm a good mother.

His words are like a balm to my soul and I make a promise, to myself at least, that I'll work to replace the fucked-up shit that Alistair said with his words.

"Thank you. I think she's pretty special too," I reply. Juan made me a steak salad that has mandarin oranges and strawberry slices in it. He added extra meat and sent along an additional container of dressing. Once I've got my salad the way I want it, I tuck into it, suddenly starved.

My nap is interrupted by the doctor who says, "Things are already looking better for you, Little Miss." I like that the healthcare providers address my child, even though she's not yet four. I think that keeping her involved, even if she doesn't fully understand what's happening, helps to keep her calm.

"Will she need another blood gas done?" I question. I won't lie; I cried when they did the first one in the emergency room. It took four nurses to hold my thirty-pound daughter down while a fifth nurse struggled to get it done. "She had a rough time in the emergency room which is why I'm asking," I explain.

He frowns then states, "It should go easier up here. One of the nurses on the IV team is a pro at getting them on children. Since we handle pediatrics on this floor, we're more geared to handling a child. But yes, to answer your question, she's going to need another one." I cringe at his words even knowing that whoever comes in will be better equipped to handle the task.

"I'll wait to go get your things until they get it done so I can help," Matt advises. His quiet assurance calms me, and I nod.

CHAPTER 8

Matt

DRIVING TO MANDIE'S HOUSE, I THINK ABOUT WHAT I just witnessed. Despite her fear because of the pain from the first blood gas test, Aria laid there and didn't move. She held onto my hand with a death grip, however, and I wince when I have to tighten my hold on the steering wheel. For such a little girl, she's got some strength. True to the doctor's word, the nurse that came in to do the blood gas draw was gentle and other than a small pinch when the needle went in, Aria didn't feel any pain.

Just before I reach the turn off to her house, I see a 'For Sale by Owner' sign in front of a farmhouse that I've admired for years. I take a chance and pull in to see if I can get any information. Parking my truck, I get out and stride up the walkway to the steps that lead to a wrap-around porch. There's someone sitting in one of the rocking chairs and I hope it's the homeowner. "Hello, I saw the sign out front and thought I'd stop," I say to the old farmer sitting there, sipping on a longneck bottle of beer.

"I know you, young man," he states, holding out his hand. "You're that fella that has a construction company with that biker club, ain'tcha?"

"Yes, sir," I reply.

"Come and sit while I tell you about the house," he commands. Even knowing that I don't have a lot of time, I still take a seat. Being single, I've lived at the clubhouse since I joined the Black Tuxedos. But I know I'll need a place for Mandie and the kids, and I want to give her something that has no memories of the past she shared with her ex.

"Did you just decide to sell it?" I question. I know I haven't seen that sign out previously and I wonder if it's destiny that today of all days, I noticed it.

"Yep, just last night. Getting to be too big for an old man like me to keep up with now that my wife has passed and the kids are grown and gone."

"I'm sorry about your wife," I say. My folks had one of those marriages and shortly after my father died, my mother did as well. Hardest fucking thing I ever went through because it was during the time I was recuperating from my injuries.

"Me and Bessie had fifty-five years together, son. We had a good life, but I guess the good Lord needed her to wrangle that kitchen up in Heaven," he replies, chuckling. "Anyhow, I'm moving to Florida near my kids. They've got one of them tiny houses or some shit on their property waiting for me so I can have my own space, but not worry about all the upkeep or something like that. At least that's what my daughter says. I can fish every day and maybe teach my grandkids a thing or two before I leave this here Earth."

"How big is the house?" I ask. From the outside, it looks massive, but never having seen it, I don't know whether the inside matches or not.

"Got five bedrooms, four bathrooms, a huge ass formal living room and dining room, a family room, a good-sized kitchen, a laundry room, a room my Bessie used for her crafting, and of course, the garage which I had a covered walkway added so she wouldn't get wet when it rained. It's out back," he states, seeing the look on my face. "All on five acres. Used to have a garden back there, but I don't have the green thumb like my Bessie did. Got a few sheds out there as well, all have electricity to them so if you're the kind of man who likes to tinker around, you'd have your own space."

This almost sounds too good to be true. I've got the money since all of our businesses are doing so well and I have minimal expenses. My truck, while a newer model, is paid for, as is my Harley. While I've got a credit card with a pretty decent balance available to me, I seldom use it and when I do, I pay it off when the bill comes. "I'm almost afraid to ask how much you're wanting," I admit.

He sighs while rubbing his hand down his face. "Son, honestly, if one of my kids wanted it, I wouldn't be selling. But they're all about the modern looking houses and don't want one that has stone fireplaces and hardwood floors. Not looking to make a killing quite frankly. That's not my style. I'm thinking one hundred and fifty thousand should be plenty."

I feel like my jaw just hit my chest. Thanks to my military pension I get every month plus what I make with the club, what he's asking for is literally chump change for me. I could buy it outright and still have more than enough to get it outfitted the way a house should be.

"You sure that's enough? I'm not about fucking anyone over."

He starts chuckling, then looks me dead in the eye. "Son, I can tell you ain't like that. Now, you want to go on inside and take a look around? Me and Bessie did a bunch of updating to the kitchen about a year before she passed. Since I don't cook, it's as clean as a whistle."

"How do you eat if you don't cook?"

"Oh, I can make me some eggs and bacon, and got that coffee habit down pat. But when it comes to regular food, I either go to The Steakhouse, hit up the diner, or allow Widow Jones to ply me with her casseroles she's constantly making for me. I can still work a microwave pretty damn good."

For some reason, knowing he's eating makes me feel better, so I nod to him as I stand up and reply, "Yeah, I'd like to check it out."

"Go on in, son. Take a look, take some pictures. I've got a good feeling."

I step to the front door and walk inside and am immediately blown away. Doing what I do for a living, there's not much I haven't seen with regard to a house, but the attention to detail that is evident is phenomenal. The rooms are painted in soft, soothing colors, with glossy white trim. I can see me living here with Mandie, the kids running around and playing. I continue my perusal, taking pictures to show her, as I make my way through the first floor. The room that the old man said was for his wife's crafting is the perfect size to set up an office for both Mandie as well as myself.

Typically, I work out of a construction trailer on whatever job site I'm at, but I still have paperwork and shit that I don't like to leave unattended. Having a dedicated office would mean that the invoices and stuff would be protected against prying eyes. So far, I've seen nothing during my tour that needs updating or repairing, which means it would be easy to move in and start living as a family.

Dumbass, you need to see if she's gonna be on board with that first. I shake my head to clear my thoughts as I make my way upstairs. Everything is neat as a pin and the bedrooms are spacious. When I come to the master bedroom, I can't help the moan that breaks free. There's a stone fireplace off to one side with a sitting area and I can see Mandie curled up with me on a plush sofa as we watch the fire and talk about our day.

As I make my way back downstairs and outside, I'm already figuring out the particulars to make this happen sooner rather than later. "Well, son, what'd you think?" the old man asks as I sit down once again.

"I like it, I want it," I inform him. "I'm sure we've got paperwork to do, so if you let me know where and when, I'll be there."

"Well, that's fantastic. I'm sure your wife will love it as much as my Bessie did."

I clear my throat before I say, "I'm not married. *Yet*."

"Ah, I see. Well, I'm sure the two of you will be happy here. I'll call my banker and get something set up, how's that?"

I hand him one of my business cards and reply, "Here's my information, just call me when it's set up."

"Will do, son, will do," he says, taking my card and putting it into the bib of his overalls.

At Mandie's, I make quick work of packing things for her and Aria, my heart breaking. The kids have everything they need and then some, but my woman? It's obvious that she's made do with what she has to have in order to make sure that her kids don't go without.

No more, I silently promise as I carry the bags out to the truck. Once that's done, I go back inside and check the fridge to make sure she has nothing that will spoil while she's with Aria at the hospital, then go ahead and take out the trash. Nothing worse than coming home and dealing with spoiled food or rotting trash and since it's within my power to take care of it for her, I do so. Then, I check all the windows and make sure everything is locked up tight before I head back to the hospital.

First, though, a trip to the big box department store is needed. I pull in, her sizes in my head, and make quick work of buying her some new clothes from the skin out. She may get pissed at me for doing it, but no woman should have to wear undergarments where the elastic is nearly in shreds. On my way to the register to check out, I spy a portable DVD player as well as some kid movies. Seeing the character on one of the cases that looks like the doll Aria has, I grab that as well as two others I think she'll like.

With everything paid for, I haul it out to my truck and grin. She's going to kill me, most likely, but at least if she does, she'll have new clothes to do it in, right?

Mandie

They took Aria down for another chest X-ray because the doctor wanted to make sure what he was hearing was accurate, so I'm sitting here, twiddling my thumbs, when Shayla and Corrie walk into the room. "Hey, y'all. What are you doing here?"

"Matt called and told Reese what happened. How is she? *Where* is she?" Corrie asks, glancing at the empty bed.

"She's getting another X-ray," I reply.

"You couldn't go with her?" Shayla questions, sitting in one of the other chairs.

"She was still somewhat sedated from her blood gas test, so they promised to hurry," I say.

"How are you holding up?" Corrie asks.

I sigh. "This isn't our first rodeo, but it's been the worst one so far. She's got pneumonia and I don't know if the asthma exacerbated that or vice versa," I admit. "I'm exhausted and scared out of my mind. She finally has insurance through the state, but I just know it's not going to cover everything and that means that I'll need to put in more hours to make a dent in what's left."

"What do you mean it won't cover everything?" Shayla questions. "I thought that Texas had a good Medicaid program."

"They do and if I had filled out the forms correctly to begin with, last year's visit, as well as Beau's birth, would have been covered. But she had a few bad episodes, plus with him being a newborn, I had my hands full. By the time I looked at the paperwork and realized I had done something wrong and fixed it, the appeal period had lapsed. They're letting me pay off the balances, but I'm positive that this hospital visit will have 'something' they won't cover that'll end up adding to what I owe them." I feel my shoulders slump, my excitement over the slight windfall I got after my last semester tuition was paid fading fast. "I'll be working until I'm ninety."

"No, you won't." Matt's voice is firm and unyielding. I glance up to see him standing in the doorway, his arms laden with bags.

"What do you mean?" I stammer out, watching as he sets the bags down that he carried into the room. I see him pull out a portable DVD player and put it on the table tray, then lay three movies alongside it. "What did you do, Matt?" I question, my voice barely above a whisper.

"Just picked a few things up is all," he replies.

"Looks like more than a few things," I admonish, glaring at him then the bags that are from the local department store. "I don't remember *anything* on my list coming from there."

He walks closer to me and leans down before he whispers, "Sweetheart, you needed some things and I wanted you to have them." Shame engulfs me at his words. I have one good bra left, which I happen to be wearing and it never crossed my mind when he went to get the stuff for me and Aria that he would see my stuff. Stupid, stupid, stupid. "Get whatever's in your head out of there, Mandie," he demands.

"Okay," I reply, my voice small. Alistair's voice is ringing in my head again.

You're such a fucking failure, Mandie. But you've always been one, so why should now be any different?

With no fanfare, he gives Corrie and Shayla a look and I hear them say, "Let us know if y'all need anything. We'll uh just go now as it looks like y'all need to talk."

124

He picks me up, sits down, then puts me back in his lap.

"Mandie, look at me," he instructs. I shake my head, too overcome with emotion to look at him. He gently tilts my head so that I'm forced to meet his eyes and what I see in his has tears flowing. "Go ahead, sweetheart, you need to get it all out before our girl gets back."

Our girl? Questions whirl in my head as I give in to the fear and terror that has held me captive since I saw my daughter's blue-tinged lips. He never says anything, just rocks me as his hands move soothingly over my back.

Finally, long minutes later, I pull back slightly and start wiping at my face. I'm not a pretty crier so I know my eyes are now swollen, my nose is red, and my cheeks are blotchy. "I'm sorry."

"For what? Being human? Fuck, Mandie, not sure how much more I can emphasize this to you, but you're a helluva good mom and breaking down is nothing to be ashamed about. I know how scared I was when I heard Aria was in the hospital. You lived it, sweetheart," he says, wiping my face of the tears I missed. Leaning closer so our lips are nearly touching, he whispers, "And you're still the prettiest fucking thing I've ever seen, sweetheart."

"How do you do that?" I question. It's as if he read my mind or something because I feel like something the dog dragged in after a bad storm, all bedraggled and pitiful.

He grins down at me before kissing my nose. "It's a gift, but it's only ever gonna work where you're concerned."

I shrug because I'm okay with that, if I honestly examine my feelings. "So, back to what you said earlier, what exactly did you mean?"

"You're not going to run yourself into the ground to pay off anything left after her insurance pays," he replies, his tone unyielding.

"Matt, I'm still paying off last winter's hospital bills," I whisper. Don't get me wrong, I'm grateful that I've got them on the state's Medicaid for kids, but even with the deductions taken by the financial aid office because of my 'hardship status', I still have an ugly balance left because I can only send them twenty-five dollars a month. With an ambulance ride, plus her actually being admitted, I know what I'll owe will be probably ridiculous.

"Okay, let's discuss this," he says. "First, let me talk and explain a few things." I nod, unsure of where he's going with everything. Aria is my responsibility, which brings to mind him calling her 'our girl' a few minutes ago, before my monumental breakdown. "I have a proposal for you." I give him a look as if to say, 'go on' but I don't verbally say a word since he said he wanted to talk first. It's then that I see a look cross his face that I can't quite decipher. He looks almost nervous, only as long as I've known him and admittedly, it's not like we're besties or anything, he's always given off an air of confident authority. I'm sure the books I read would call him an alpha, but he has a streak of gentleness and kindness in him that probably isn't part of the alpha code.

At that thought, I giggle a bit. Here he is trying to have a serious conversation with me and I'm off in my head considering whether or not he's an alpha. "You okay, sweetheart?" he questions.

"Yeah, I'm sorry," I reply. "Carry on," I advise, waving my hand. He takes it in his and kisses my palm and I melt.

"I bought a house today on the way back to the hospital." I feel my brows raise to my hairline and he shakes his head. "Well, I'm waiting to hear from the man, but that farmhouse not too far from where you live now went up for sale and after I went through it a few hours ago, I decided it was perfect for us." He pulls out his phone and opens up his photos, then thumbs to the beginning before he holds it in front of me. "Here, look."

I take the phone and start slowly looking at the pictures he took. The house is humongous, and I can't understand why Matt would want to rattle around in something that huge all by himself. "It's beautiful," I murmur, my finger touching what is apparently the master bedroom. I can see a stone fireplace and imagine myself curled up with my e-reader and something warm to drink while a fire flickers behind the fire screen.

"I bought it for us; you, me, the kids."

Now my jaw is practically on the floor. "You what?" I look around the room to see if there are any hidden cameras, just waiting for someone to jump out and tell me I'm being punked.

"Well, you know I live at the clubhouse now and it's not appropriate for little kids to grow up there. Sure, it'll be okay if there's a late night or something like that, but not as a full-time home."

"Matt, I have a house," I state. I mean, he just fixed and upgraded my damn deck, for fuck's sake.

"That you lived in with that fucker, the one who hurt you. This place would be ours, sweetheart, where we can make memories for our family."

"Our family?" I swear, if the *Twilight Zone* music or the theme song from that other show I used to watch as a kid, *The Outer Limits*, starts playing, I will walk my ass to information and commit myself to the psych ward.

"Our family," he repeats, his voice soft, but still no less firm than it was a few minutes ago. "You and I are happening. I get that we don't know each other all that well, but we've got plenty of time to get there. What I'm proposing is that as soon as Aria gets released from the hospital, we get married so I can put y'all on my insurance with the club. I know you're probably not ready for a physical relationship with any man just yet, and there are things I need to share with you, but this way, you won't work yourself into an early grave."

"So, a marriage of convenience?" I ask. I'm not sure how I feel about it, but I know that sometimes, the couple actually falls for one another. Old tauntings of Alistair's try to surface but I squash them down. This isn't about him; it's about me and Matt. "How is that fair to you, Matt?"

"I get a beautiful woman as my wife and old lady, and two adorable kids that I'll raise as if they were my own."

"What about more kids? Would you want more, someday?"

He rakes one of his hands through his hair and says, "I've got some things to tell you, but would rather wait until we had a bit more privacy. That's not off the table, but I get that initially, we'll kind of be doing shit backwards. Most people meet, date, decide they want each other and jump into bed, then either live together for a while or just get married. We'd be getting married and then learning more about each other."

"You would do that for me — us?" I question. "What if I'm a serial killer or a bank robber on the lam or something?"

He starts chuckling and is soon laughing so hard, his head is thrown back. I watch in amazement because he's a good-looking man, but when he laughs, he moves into a completely different stratosphere. "You're fucking adorable, you know that right?" he manages to ask between fits of laughter.

"I'm a bit concerned that you think this is funny. It *could* be true, you know."

"First of all, if you were either of those things, you wouldn't have your kids. Second of all, Juan and Maria are excellent judges of character, as all of us in the club are, and there's no way he'd allow his beloved daughter to babysit for you. Lastly, sweetheart, if you were a bank robber, you were a pretty terrible one because as hard as you work, you don't really have a lot to your name." I feel myself bristle at his words; I may not have a lot, but what I have is mine and I've busted my ass for every single thing since Alistair left me high and dry. "Sweetheart, I wasn't casting aspersions on you or your ability to do anything. Just an observation. I know how hard you work, it's evident in how well you keep that place you live, despite the fact that I think a strong wind would carry it away and by how your kids have everything they need, as well as quite a few of their wants from what I could tell."

I deflate at his words. Here he is, pretty much offering me everything on a silver platter and I want to fuss about his choice of words? That's kind of rude and if Mama T were here, she'd be giving me her signature look. "I'm sorry, Matt. I don't mean to get defensive."

"Never apologize for sticking up for yourself, pretty girl, even to me. So, what do you say?" he asks.

CHAPTER 9

Mandie

I LOOK AT HIM BUT DON'T SAY ANYTHING, MY MIND whirling with the information overload he's just released on me. I mean, I'm attracted to him, sure, but what if he figures out I'm not all that? Of course, he made a lot of sense too. Sure, we'd be starting out a bit backward from most relationships, but people have gotten into them before with less in common. Right? I already know a lot about him from how he's treated me, as well as the fact that when he heard about Aria, he came right to the hospital and other than running to get a few things, he seems to be sticking around.

"You're overthinking things, Mandie," he murmurs when I remain silent.

"Am I? I mean, you'd be taking on a hell of a lot, Matt," I retort. "Two kids, me... that's quite a bit to ask anyone to take on."

"How so?" he asks.

Instead of answering him, I remind myself that I decided to grab the brass ring with both hands. "Well, unless I miss my guess, you've never been married before, correct?" He nods in agreement, so I continue. "I'm a raging lunatic once a month; chocolate isn't safe within a ten-mile radius. That something you can live with?"

"I'll go buy stock in your favorite brand today if I need to," he replies, his face serious even though his eyes are twinkling.

"Then there's the fact that Beau hasn't even started walking yet, but if he's anything like Aria was, nothing will be safe. Of course, she'll eventually become a teenager as well. See what I mean? I don't see what you'll get out of the deal."

"You." His softly spoken word takes the wind out of my sails, especially when he tips my chin up with his finger and cradles my face in his hand. Before I can respond, his lips are descending toward mine and I feel the softest kiss imaginable while his thumb lightly strokes my cheek. Even though he keeps the kiss light and not overly invasive given where we are, I still feel as though I've been branded down to the marrow of my bones.

I pull back slightly and ask, "Is that enough?"

"Yeah." His voice is huskier, and he pulls me close again only this kiss is anything but soft and light. I feel a fire start burning deep in my gut, one that I never knew was there, and my hands move to cup his head, my fingers roaming up and down his body in an attempt to learn his physique.

Finally needing air, I pull back slightly and say, "Yes."

"Yes?"

"Yes, I'll marry you. It may not be conventional, but most of my life hasn't been, you know? We'll figure it out as we go along." At my words, he kisses me again and desire unlike anything I've ever experienced before engulfs me, causing me to squirm on his lap.

"Guess you need this then," he replies, once again pulling back slightly. He reaches into his pocket and pulls out a simple engagement ring. "It's not much, but I had limited options available seeing as how I wanted to get back here to y'all," he says, slipping it on my finger.

"It's beautiful," I state, looking down at the silver band with a diamond solitaire in the center. I've never had much jewelry-wise, just a few pieces that were my mother's, but when Alistair left, he stole them.

I'm about to say something else when I hear the unmistakable sound of giggles coming toward the room. Glancing up, I see Aria riding in the wheelchair they took her down in, a princess crown on her head and a blanket wrapped around her shoulders like a cape. She's got her hand up and is waving to people as she passes them. "She's something else," Matt says, looking at the door.

"That she is," I reply, standing to greet her and the nurse. "How did she do?" I ask.

"She was perfect," the nurse says as she helps get Aria back into her bed before she reconnects all the tubes where they belong. "The doctor should have the results shortly."

"Thank you." I look at Aria and see that despite her merriment, she's wiped out. "How about you take a nap, sweetie?"

"I don't like naps, Mommy, but I is very tired right now," she admits.

"Just a little one, okay?" I lean down and kiss her forehead, grateful that she seems to have broken the slight fever she did have when she first arrived.

We end up staying two additional days before the doctor releases us to go home. As I pack up all the things that have made their way to the hospital courtesy of not only Matt but also Shayla and Corrie, I keep glancing at my finger where my diamond sparkles. We're going today from here to the courthouse to get married. Not sure how he managed it, but he was able to get our marriage license despite me not being with him and I suspect it had more to do with the fact that he's a member of the club than anything.

Juan, Maria and Ollie are meeting us there with Beau and will stand up as our witnesses. I did ask Matt if he wanted anyone from the club, but he said they would be good enough. He also said if I wanted, we could have a fancy wedding down the road, but I'm okay with us going to the courthouse.

Once I have everything packed up, I slip into Aria's bathroom to try and make myself presentable. Even though I slept in her bed with her, I still have deep circles under my eyes and lament the fact that I don't have any makeup.

"Are you ready, sweetheart?" Matt asks, coming into the room. He already took one load of our things down to his truck while they have Aria getting one last X-ray. At this rate, she's going to start glowing. I'm just glad she's feeling better.

"Yeah," I reply, walking out with yet more things that were stashed in the bathroom. "How is it we were here less than a week and yet, we have all this stuff?"

He chuckles as he takes what I'm holding and puts it all into yet another duffle bag. "Probably because everyone kept bringing things to y'all," he replies, leaning in to kiss me. "You ready for this?" he asks, his finger stroking my ring.

I take a deep breath and let it out before saying, "Yes. Still think you're getting the raw end of it all, but no take-backs." He grins and kisses my forehead before turning to the door where I hear Aria singing.

"We're all ready to go, Mom," the nurse says as she brings Aria into the room. "I'll wheel the princess down if you want to go get the vehicle."

"You walk with her, sweetheart, I'll pull the truck around," Matt states. Looking at the nurse, he asks, "Do I pull around to the front?"

"Yes, sir," she replies.

He leans in and kisses my forehead then ruffles Aria's hair. "I'll see you two downstairs in a few minutes." He then grabs all the bags and walks out the door and I feel my heartbeat speed up. I have no clue what the future holds and I'm anxious as hell, but I suspect this man, who has already turned my world on its axis, is going to show me what it really means to be loved.

Matt

I pull the truck around to the front and get out to wait. When I see Mandie and Aria, I open the doors before I scoop Aria up, set her in the car seat and get her buckled. Once she's squared away, I kiss her head and say, "I'm glad you're feeling better, sweetheart."

"Me too, Mr. Matt. Is we going to gets married now?" she asks.

"Yes, we are," Mandie replies. I grin as I make sure her door is shut tight, then walk around the front of the truck and slide into the driver's seat. Leaning over, I gently tug Mandie toward me and kiss her. "So, you got car seats for your truck too?" she asks. I smirk at her as I nod, then put the truck in gear.

"Why is you kissing my mommy?" Aria questions.

I chuckle. She never stops asking questions and is inquisitive as fuck, just like JJ and Meli are. "Because I like kissing your mommy," I state. And judging from the tightness of my jeans, my dick does as well.

The trip to the courthouse doesn't take very long since our town is barely more than a couple of red lights. I park and repeat the process of getting Aria out but when I attempt to keep carrying her, she says, "I wants to walk, Mr. Matt. Please lets me." How the fuck can I resist this little three-year-old cutie? I put her down and hold out my hand for her to take. She grasps my huge, calloused hand in her dainty fingers and grins up at me. Shaking my head, I reach for Mandie's hand and lace our fingers together.

It feels so fucking right, despite how backwards we're doing things. We walk into the courthouse and my jaw nearly drops. Juan, Maria, Olive and Beau are standing off to the side, which I wholly expected. But standing with them are my brothers as well as the old ladies. When I look at Reese, he states, "We'll always have y'alls back, Matt."

"How did you find out?" I ask. He gives a nod down to Aria, who is currently hugging Juan and chattering to Beau.

"Let's do this thing," Corrie says, hugging Mandie.

Reese leans in and says, "Y'all are coming back to the clubhouse once we're through here. No arguments. We got Mandie's cut ready and waiting there."

I just shake my head because it doesn't bother me one bit that not only will she be my old lady, but I'll have her tied to me legally as well. "Where do we need to go?" Mandie asks.

"Through here," Shayla says, pointing to a sign. As a group, we move into Courtroom A, where an older man is sitting there. Based on his robes, I'm going with the thought that he's the judge who'll be marrying us today. A thrill shoots through me; after Jessa, I never expected to be in this position. I won't say that I love Mandie, but I think we've got a good foundation started with being friends. I respect the hell out of what she's managed to accomplish on her own and am grateful that she found Juan and his family.

The judge stands and walks over to us. "So, who am I marrying today?" he asks.

"Us," Aria says, pointing at me, her mom, Beau and herself. Mandie smiles and I realize that I haven't talked to her about eventually adopting the kids as my own. *Later*, I promise myself.

"Actually, it's him and me," Mandie replies, holding up our joined hands.

"Well, I see you've got plenty of witnesses. Family?" he questions.

"Absolutely. Maybe not by blood, but family isn't always about that," I state.

"You're correct, young man," the judge says.

The ceremony doesn't take long and before I know it, the judge pronounces us husband and wife.

I have a wife, I think as I gently kiss her. Her soft smile after I pull back has me stroking my hand down her cheek.

"Clubhouse," Reese calls out after hugging Mandie and slapping me on the back. Maria is busy taking pictures of us all and I make a mental note to see if I can find someone who can take family pictures of the four of us to start our new life.

CHAPTER 10

Mandie

I'M MARRIED.

We head to the clubhouse, the kids chattering in the back of the truck, and I can't stop looking at the wedding band that now sits on my left ring finger. That day he went shopping, he got everything at once; a fact that still blows me away. "You're awfully quiet over there," he murmurs, glancing at me.

"Still can't believe we did this," I reply.

"No take-backs," he teases, using the words I said to him a few days ago.

"No take-backs," I promise. Deciding I need to say more, I continue. "I promise that I'll always be honest, and I'll hold your secrets as if they are my own. I won't stray and if we have an argument of any kind, I promise to talk it out until we reach a solution or a compromise."

He nods, saying, "This is new for me too, sweetheart. Been a long time since I've been in any kind of relationship, and while I know we're just starting, I think we've got a good foundation already."

"I think so too," I reply, looking at him. He winks at me and I feel myself blushing. I wonder if he's going to want sex right away. The thought doesn't freak me out as much as I thought it might, but I'm still nervous about him seeing me naked with all my faults and flaws on display.

"Whatever you're overthinking about, you need to stop, sweetheart," he advises.

I shake my head. "You're doing it again," I retort.

"What's that?"

"Somehow, you knew I was in my head about something," I reply.

"You get a look on your face when that happens," he says. I'm about to reply when he pulls up to the clubhouse. Putting the truck in park, he motions for me to stay put, then he gets Beau out and walks around to the rear passenger side to unbuckle Aria and help her down. Once they're taken care of, he opens my door and helps me out, kissing me after I'm standing in front of him. "Okay, let's see why they needed us here."

I take Aria's hand and despite him carrying Beau, he still manages to pull me into his side with his arm around my shoulders. The weight gives me a sense of peace and security I haven't known in years. When he opens the door and I see the sign that's hanging from the ceiling, I start crying.

He hurriedly passes Beau off to Olive, who came over to us and pulls me into his arms. "Shh, sweetheart, it's okay," he whispers.

"N-n-no one has ever done as much for me as y'all have," I stammer out. "I wasn't expecting this at all."

"They're family, Mandie," he replies. "And since you're my wife and old lady, they're yours as well. They want to celebrate our beginning which I think is fucking fantastic."

I manage to get my tears to stop and look up at him. Being this close, I can see the sincerity in his gaze. "I'm good, Matt. It just surprised me is all." I hear the clicking of nails and glance to my left to see his dog coming toward us, three others behind him. "We've got company," I say, giggling.

"Champ, Bosco, Louie, Duke," he replies, pointing to each one. "Since we're all together and not stressing, they're roaming right now."

A thought crosses my mind and I ask, "Where are we staying?"

"We'll have to stay at your place until I get the details on the house finalized," he admits. "Shouldn't be more than a few weeks, though. It doesn't need any renovations and in fact, the current owner wants me to bring you by because he's willing to let us keep whatever furnishings we want. The only thing I insist on is a new bedroom suite."

"We're going to share a room?" I whisper. I mean, our relationship isn't conventional and outside of the few kisses we've shared, he's given no indication about his expectations regarding physical intimacy.

He tilts my chin and leans even closer. "We may not be there yet, but yes, you're my wife and I'm your husband so we'll be by one another." His voice is firm, yet kind and I nod.

"Okay, Matt," I murmur.

"Can we party now?" Aria asks, interrupting our moment. I suspect that'll happen frequently, because she's always on the go. Her enforced rest during her hospital stay nearly drove me crazy, because the steroids hyped her already exuberant personality up even more. When she was finally allowed out of the bed, we spent a lot of time walking around the floor just to try and wear her out.

"Absolutely," Matt states, drawing me further into the room where I see balloons and streamers decorating the walls and tables. One long table is off to the side with covered pans and I instinctively know that Juan and Maria made the food.

The next few hours are spent eating and talking with everyone, with Maria constantly snapping pictures. When she stops by me, I ask, "Can you email me the pictures you've taken today?"

"Absolutely, sweet girl. You ready for some cake?"

Cake? We have cake? *Score!*

"Is that a serious question, Maria? By the way, I can't thank y'all enough for taking care of Beau for me."

"It's what family does, *mija*," she replies, kissing my cheek. Matt comes over and wraps his arms around me from behind and I lean into his embrace.

"We've got cake, Matt," I tell him.

"Well, every good party has cake," he replies, chuckling. He walks me over to the table where a beautiful wedding cake is sitting. I start laughing when I see the motorcycle on top, with a groom wearing a cut and the bride in jeans and a long-sleeved shirt.

"That's so cute!" I exclaim.

"Got something for you, sweetheart," Matt states.

Matt

I know our wedding isn't conventional by society's standards but I'm a biker and we don't do all the glitz and glamor as a rule. Seeing how relaxed Mandie is with my brothers, as well as the old ladies, makes me realize that despite my concern over our courthouse marriage, she's perfectly content. I walk over behind the table and withdraw a box, then hand it over to Mandie. "Go ahead, open it before we cut the cake," I advise.

I watch as she removes the top and opens the tissue paper inside. Her slight gasp makes me smile; I don't think she realized that she would get a 'property of' cut when she agreed to be mine. "It's beautiful," she whispers, her voice reverent as she pulls the cut out, her hands stroking the leather. A vision of her wearing nothing but that while she's astride me comes to mind and I feel my jeans tighten.

Down, boy. Now's not the time, dammit!

"Let me help you, sweetheart," I murmur, taking the cut from her hands. I want to see my name on her, something I never thought would happen in my life. I carefully slide it on and am rewarded when she smiles up at me. I've noticed that despite the unconventionality of our relationship, she's more relaxed these days. "It looks good, Mandie," I tell her, leaning in to kiss her lips.

"I can't wait to go riding," she confesses.

"You've ridden before?" I feel jealousy streak through me at the thought of her holding onto another man.

"My grandpa belonged to a riding club when I was a little girl and he used to take me for rides. I was little then, maybe six? But I remember how free I felt, and I imagine that I'll feel the same way now that I'm all grown up, right?"

I grin down at her, my ire now gone. "Can't wait to have you on my bike, pretty girl."

"Alright, alright, can we cut the cake? Some of us pregnant women need that goodness in our bellies!" Corrie calls out. Mandie starts to giggle and I vow that I'll give her plenty of things to laugh about in our life together.

"Guess that's our cue, sweetheart," I tell her. With little fuss, we soon have the cake cut and have fed each other a piece. She doesn't smash my piece into my face; instead, after I take the proffered bite, she swipes her thumb across my lower lip to catch a crumb. The gentleness behind her touch is oddly erotic and I find myself wishing we were at that point, because I'd love nothing more than to scoop her up and carry her to my room.

"Oh my God, I've died and gone to Heaven," Shayla moans out between bites.

"Think you said that last night too, baby," Nick asserts, smirking.

She smacks him on the arm while all the adults burst into laughter. Thankfully, the kids are all clueless. I glance over and see Beau, sitting in a high chair, covered from head to toe in frosting. "How does that even happen?" I ask, nudging Mandie and pointing over to him.

"You should've seen when Ollie planted the garden! I came home and he was covered in topsoil. She washed his face and hands to feed him, but he looked like Pigpen and oh my goodness, the tub! It took two baths to get him clean again."

"We've got a hose in the back, it might be easier," Reese states.

"We could set up the sprinkler for the kids, it's nice out today," Corrie adds.

"Yay, sprinklers!" Aria yells, causing JJ and Meli to start hollering.

"I got it," Porter says, standing. "C'mon, y'all, let's go play outside." The kids follow him and I gotta give my brother props because he picks Beau up, high chair and all and carries him out to the back of the clubhouse.

We spend the next several hours watching the kids play, chatting with my brothers and their old ladies. "Mandie, when can you start doing the bookkeeping?" Corrie asks.

"Any time you're ready for me," she replies. "I've only got my final to take and I'm done."

"Good. I'll get the stuff ordered that you need and bring it over so we can get you all set up."

"Corrie, let's wait until we get into the new house, that way it doesn't have to be moved twice," I advise. "That'll give me time to get the desks in the room we're going to use as an office."

"That works too."

"Mommy, I is tired," Aria states, coming up and climbing onto Mandie's lap.

"It's been a busy day and we did just get you out of the hospital. Let's get our stuff together and head home, okay?" Mandie questions.

"You have the next week off," Juan advises.

"Juan, I need to..."

"No, you don't, sweetheart," I tell her. "Aria still isn't one hundred percent and you need to start packing your place up for when we move."

"Next week is soon enough for you to come back. Besides, your regular customers will be so happy, they'll probably throw money at you," Juan says, laughing.

"So the new girl is having challenges?" Mandie questions.

"Just a few," Maria says. "With Shona now gone, the new girl, Amalia, has been pulling more shifts. If we could get her to understand that she doesn't need to flirt with every man who walks into the place, she'd do much better."

"It's because she used to work at a strip club," Olive replies.

"How do you know that?" I ask, my curiosity aroused.

"I asked her the other day. Mama was home with Beau, and I came into the restaurant to help Papa. I saw what she was doing and finally, I asked her. When she told me that, I told her to tone it down because she was pissing off the women and that was why she wasn't getting many tips."

"You told her that?" Mandie inquires. "Good. Because she obviously didn't hear me when I said the same damn thing. If you're going to be friendly, that's fine, but don't ignore the women and focus solely on the men. It's not right and it's not appropriate."

"I may need to rethink her employment," Juan mumbles.

"Maybe she could go on hostess duty," Maria suggests. "The increase in her hourly pay would make up the difference in what she would make in tips."

"Considering she's not really making any tips, it would be a raise," Olive asserts, giggling.

With both kids rounded up, I stand there, my arm around Mandie and look at everyone. "Can't thank y'all enough for today. It means more than you'll ever know."

"You're family," Reese states. "Both of you, as well as the kids. It's what family does." I nod and call Champ over from where he was lounging. He and the other three dogs are worn out thanks to running and playing with the kids all day. He meanders over to us and I give a wave before turning and walking back through the clubhouse.

It's time to take my family home.

CHAPTER 11

Mandie

I KNOW I'M QUIET ON THE RIDE TO THE HOUSE, BUT so many things are swirling in my head that I can't voice them. Matt took his cut off and helped me take mine off before we got into the truck; I need to know why. I'm worried about tonight too. Will we have a typical wedding night? Or was he telling the truth when he said it would happen when it happened? I know I'm attracted to him; the way my body reacts whenever he's around clued me in to that fact. Plus, with all the time we've spent together these past few days, I have found that I genuinely like him. We have a lot of common interests, something that Alistair and I didn't have, and his insight into so many things has given me new ideas about how to handle stuff.

"Today's been a good day," he says, taking my hand in his and lacing our fingers together. I glance down at them, loving how mine seems to fit into his just right. The difference in our skin tones is telling; he's tanned, and his hands have that rough feel that I equate with a man who works hard, while mine are pale and much, much softer.

"Yeah it has. I still can't believe we're married," I reply.

"I'd say me either, but that would be a lie. I've always been attracted to you," he admits. "Just didn't think it was reciprocated. Otherwise, I would've asked you out a long time ago."

"I'm glad things worked out the way they did because if you had, I probably wouldn't have been ready and might have said no," I state. "I'm still concerned that you got the worst part of it all."

"Not from where I'm sitting." He glances over at me and grins. "A beautiful woman and two adorable kids, what else could a man ask for?"

I roll my eyes at him and he chuckles. "You didn't say you had a few screws loose, Matt," I tease. "I resemble a troll in the morning."

"Prettiest troll I've ever seen then."

"I have a question though, why did we take our cuts off before we got in the truck?"

"Because we don't wear them in vehicles, only when we're not in them or on our bikes."

I think about it and say, "Is it a respect thing or something?"

"That's exactly what it is. We can wear our shirts that have our patch on them in vehicles and such, but not our cuts."

"I don't want to misstep so if there's anything else I need to know, please tell me," I implore.

"You never pat someone wearing their cut on the back without announcing your presence. Basically, treat your cut like it's our American flag. It doesn't touch the ground, you don't wear someone else's, and whenever we go somewhere on the bike and we're in another club's territory, you remove it as a sign of respect toward the dominant club in the area."

"So many things to learn," I murmur. "I don't want to do anything to bring shame to you or the club, Matt."

"Anything you do *is* a reflection on me, but I'm not worried and you shouldn't be either. You're always kind to others, as well as respectful, Mandie. You'll be just fine."

Deciding a subject change is in order, I ask, "When will the house be ready?"

"Mr. Smithers' daughter has come up and they are currently packing the stuff he wants to keep, as well as dividing up sentimental items. He's thinking maybe a month."

"Will you be okay with us staying at the house that long?" I worry my lower lip while I wait for his answer. I know he doesn't like it simply because of who lived there before, but I suspect it has more to do with the treatment I received at another man's hand than anything else.

"I'll be fine, sweetheart. What do you say about us getting the kids out and into a bath. Aria looks ready to drop." I glance back at my sweet girl and see her slumped in her car seat, her eyes half-closed, Poppy clutched in her arms. Her color is good, though, so I know she didn't overexert herself. Still, she did just get out of the hospital today, so I know she's likely wiped out.

"Sounds like a plan," I reply. I'll worry about bedtime later.

Matt

I know she's worrying about later tonight, but I'm not sure how to allay her fears. As we get the kids out of the truck and into the house, I wait outside while Champ does his thing. "Good boy," I state when he finally runs over to me, tail wagging. "Let's go see how we can help." His tail thumps against the door jamb as we walk inside, and I grin. Each night that I've been visited by Jackal, Champ has woken me up and the time to go back to sleep has lessened.

Once inside, I make sure the house is locked up, then head in search of my wife.

My wife.

Two words that I never thought would be in my vocabulary. The possibilities are endless and I'm anticipating a time when we're together intimately. I know I need to tell her about my injuries, but tonight isn't that time. "Here, let me get him," I say, taking a sleeping Beau from her arms. Looking down at the little boy who is his mother's mini-me in male form, I grin. "He sure looks different." He's clean, for one thing, but the play at the clubhouse has his cheeks rosy.

"He'll be back to his normal messy self tomorrow, trust me," she replies, giggling. I take him into the room that the two kids share and lay him in his crib. Aria is already asleep on her little toddler bed and I grin. Once Beau is settled, I walk over to the little girl and crouch down to tuck her in better. As I lightly run my finger down her cheek, her eyes flutter open.

"I is glad you married us today, Mr. Matt," her sleepy voice says, causing my heart to lurch.

"So am I, sweetheart. So am I," I manage to choke out through the lump in my throat. Once I'm sure that both kids are settled, I stand and see Mandie against the wall, tears shimmering in her eyes. Walking over to her, I cup her face in my hands. "You okay, sweetheart?"

"They say that animals and kids are a good judge of character. I think I hit the lottery," she murmurs, looking up at me.

"So did I," I reply, leaning in and kissing her. "Why don't you do whatever it is that you do to get ready for bed? We can wind down a bit and talk."

"Okay," she says. I watch her scurry into the master bedroom, then hear drawers opening and closing before the bathroom door closes. Satisfied that all is right in my world for the time being, I head into the kitchen and grab a beer.

CHAPTER 12

Mandie

As I go through my nightly routine, I can't stop looking at my rings. Growing up and seeing the love my parents shared, I dreamed of a time that I would have something like they did. When they died and I went into foster care, I shelved those dreams and focused on my grief. I'm so grateful that I got Mama T because she knew that the broken-hearted teenager who walked through her front door didn't care about anything. If not for her, I don't know if I would have done well in school or taken another path. "I'm married, Mama T," I whisper, stroking my moisturizer over my face. "Can you believe it? Me? You'd love my babies. I'm sorry I didn't listen to you about Alistair, but if not for him, I wouldn't have Aria and Beau, so something that ended badly with respect to him had two beautiful results." The grief that was a constant pain when she first died shortly after I had Aria has lessened, but times like right now, I wish she was still here in the physical sense. I'd like to think she would be proud of how I've managed to rise above the shit that Alistair gave me.

Once I'm done, I take a few minutes to give myself a pep talk. I have no clue what's about to happen when I walk through that door. Finally ready, I open the bedroom door to find Matt already in the bed leaning against the headboard. I see a bottle of water on my nightstand and notice that he's idly flipping channels with the remote. I start giggling and he looks at me. "What?" he asks, his eyes taking in everything about my appearance.

I point to the remote and he grins. "I think it's hard-wired in every man's DNA to find and hold a remote," I reply.

His bark of laughter increases my giggles as I slip into the bed. He's a big guy and I only have a full-size bed, so as soon as I'm in, I feel surrounded. I glance at him and he smirks at me. "You're probably right and we definitely need a bigger bed, sweetheart."

"You think?" I retort. As soon as the words leave my mouth, I cringe. Alistair hated when I talked back. *He's not like that*, my brain reminds me.

He slowly turns toward me, his moves cautious. "Mandie, you've gotta know, I'll never raise my hand to you in anger. *Ever.*" His voice is vehement, nearly angry in tone, but I understand regardless.

"I'm sorry. Old habit," I mumble, suddenly embarrassed. Matt has never given me a reason to think otherwise, so why now am I reacting in this manner?

"Come here, sweetheart," he says, opening his arms. I scoot closer, which doesn't take much, and find myself pulled into his side. I notice he's got a T-shirt and sleep pants on and worry that he'll get too hot. His hand strokes my arm and side, and I relax further into his embrace. If we never have anything more, I could be content.

"I'm good, Matt," I finally say. I hear a thump-thump sound from his side of the bed and glance over to see Champ lying there. "He's a really beautiful dog."

"He picked me, believe it or not, but I agree. Smart as hell, too," he replies, kissing my forehead.

"I noticed that when we were at the clubhouse, he was watching you, but he also stayed close to Aria." Beau, not so much as we kept him somewhat confined to the playpen while the older kids ran around like a herd of elephants.

"Kind of suspect that he picked up on the fact she's not completely healthy yet," he states. "I like that because even though he's a dog, it means we've got more eyes on them."

"I wonder if he'll keep Beau from getting so dirty," I muse.

"Considering that the other day at the job site he was rolling around in a mud puddle, I highly doubt it. Guess I better pick up more dog shampoo because I suspect those two will be bathing frequently. Maybe I should put an outdoor shower in at the new place, what do you think?"

He sounds so serious, but I catch his lips tilted up and I can't stop the laughter that bursts forth. The visuals I have of my little guy and his dog rolling around like pigs in mud soon has tears flowing from my eyes. "They're going to think it's a match made in Heaven," I finally gasp out.

"There won't be a dull moment, I'm sure." He slowly slides us down on the bed, so our heads are on the pillows, then turns so we're face-to-face. "Y'know, since I got hurt and was discharged from the military, not one single woman has elicited any kind of physical reaction."

My brow wrinkles and I ask, "What do you mean? You've been out awhile now, right?"

Matt

Honest to God, I never intended to have this discussion tonight of all nights, yet I want her to know me, all of me. "I went in right out of high school and left my fiancé at home waiting. We had dated through high school and were planning to get married during one of my leaves. Except, I got hurt pretty badly, and the rest of the men in my unit were killed. It took a while for me to get rehabbed enough to come home." I reach over and grab my water, downing half the bottle before I put it back. This next part is so fucking hard to relive, even now, a decade later. But she needs to get how freaking important she is because no one elicited any kind of response in my body until she came along.

"You don't have to continue if it's too difficult." Her soft voice wafts over my soul as her hand soothes me.

"No, you need to know," I insist. I take a deep breath and say, "I came home and initially she was excited to see me. She wasn't able to visit me when I was still overseas and when I got back, she was busy with work." Personally, I think she could've tried harder because I know I would've, but I've come to realize that Jessa is somewhat self-centered. "We uh, we went to bed that night and things were going well until she saw my scars." Mandie leans back and I watch her eyes scan me.

"You have scars? I don't see them," she admits.

"Because I'm clothed, sweetheart. The explosion from the RPG that was launched at us caused injuries to the left side of my body. She said a bunch of shit about how I was a monster and repulsive and well, I ended up developing what the doctors said was idiopathic erectile dysfunction."

"She did what?" Mandie whisper-shrieks. "What a bitch! You were alive and that should've been the most important thing, not the fact that you have scars, for fuck's sake." I hide my grin because she tries not to swear, so I know that she's incensed. A small part of me loves that she's upset on my behalf and I'm man enough to own that. "Damn, Matt, I'm so sorry. That was cruel and insensitive of her. What happened then?"

"I left and bounced around a bit until Reese tracked me down and gave me a home with the Black Tuxedos. Been here ever since."

"How did you get involved in construction?"

"My pops. He had his own company and as soon as I could walk, he took me with him. I had my own kid-sized tools and would 'help' him. Until I left for the military, I worked with him every chance I had. He taught me everything I know. When I finally got out, we decided as a club to make that one of our businesses."

"My foster mom, Mama T, added on to what my mom had already taught me as far as cooking and stuff."

"Looking forward to tasting more of your cooking, sweetheart. If that sandwich you made me is any indication, I'll definitely enjoy it," I tell her. I see her hiding a yawn and lean over to turn out the light. "Why don't we get some sleep, sweetheart? It's been an eventful few days, especially for you, and I know you've got to be exhausted."

She snuggles even closer to me and nods. "I'm not sure if it's my body realizing that I'm home or what, but suddenly I can't keep my eyes open." I lean down and capture her lips with mine.

"Good night, Mandie. Sleep well," I whisper against her lips. Someday, she'll be exhausted for an entirely different reason.

CHAPTER 13

Mandie

It's been a few weeks since Matt and I got married and we've settled in like, well, an old married couple. I giggle to myself as I swap the clothes from the washer into the dryer, then start another load. He's at church right now, something that he explained they do at least once a week, so I figured I'd do the laundry and get it caught up for at least a few hours. Aria gave us a bad night and I'm worn out. With both kids now lying down napping, I decide to join them, Champ at my side. "C'mon, boy, let's see if we can get a little shuteye before those two wake back up." He wags his tail and follows me to our room, where I crawl over into the middle and pull Matt's pillow close. Surprisingly, living with him has been easy. I hate comparing, but Alistair was messy, and Matt is so neat, it's almost freaky. However, it's had some positive benefits because now Aria makes sure that she picks up all of their toys at the end of the day. I

169

caught her telling Beau, who was just babbling as he crawled around, that it was important to make sure that everything was put away where it belonged so they could find it again.

"I'm happy," I whisper out loud. We still haven't had sex, but he's very free with his touches and kisses. I also haven't seen the scars he mentioned on our wedding night, but honestly, no matter how bad they are, I'm not going to give that first shit. He's more than any scar and he has come to mean so much to me, even in this short time, that his actions supersede his looks.

Champ woofs softly at me and I grin. "Everything okay with the kids?" I ask. He always checks on them when they're laying down. He woofs again, his tail wagging, before he plops down onto the doggy bed next to Matt's side. We're supposed to move into the new house this weekend and I'm excited because that means we can set the office up. I got my diploma in the mail the other day too and Matt said that once we got everything moved in, we'd be having a party at the clubhouse to celebrate both events. They sure like to get together, but I'm not going to complain. I've been alone for so long that having friends now is awesome. Not a day goes by, even the ones where I work, that I don't talk to one of the other old ladies, and Shayla has handed the clothes that are too small for Meli down to Aria. Plus, she's going to teach me how to sew.

I fall asleep while creating a mental to-do list of everything that's left to pack before we move.

Whining wakes me up as I slowly open my eyes. "Champ?" I call out, hearing him bark. Coughing, I sit up in the bed and look around, unsure of what I'm hearing. "Smoke? Why am I smelling smoke?" I murmur as I get out of bed to investigate. As I make my way to the kids' room, I can see the hallway engulfed in flames and Champ is standing in their doorway, frantically barking. I realize then why I'm smelling smoke as well as what the noise itself was — the smoke detectors.

"Aria, Beau!" I cry out, running toward their room. As I breach the doorway, Champ by my side, I see that they're still asleep. Knowing I don't have much time, I race over to Beau's crib and scoop him up, blanket and all. "Aria, sweetie, wake up," I yell. When she opens her eyes, I notice she's coughing and realize the smoke has gotten that much worse. "Hold onto my hand and Champ's collar," I instruct.

"Mommy, it's hot," she wheezes out.

"I know, baby. We've got to get out of here." I look back down the hall and take a deep breath because we're going to literally have to go through fire to get out of the house. "Don't let go, sweetheart." I'm terrified right now, but I have to save my babies. Beau starts crying as we move down the hall. It's slower going than I'd like, and I wish I was able to pick both of them up. When I hear crackling, I decide to chance it and lean over and scoop her up on my other hip. "We've got to run, Aria. Hold on to Mommy," I instruct.

Long scary moments pass as I maneuver us past the fire and out the front door, Champ right by my side. The new SUV that Matt bought for me is far enough back that I decide to set the kids inside while I call for help. "Mommy, you is on fire," Aria says once I've put her down next to the SUV. I quickly open the door, thankful that I forgot to lock it, and motion for her to get inside while I put Beau in his car seat.

"Buckle him up, Aria," I command. I don't know if it's because of the adrenaline rushing through me or what, but I don't feel any pain as I drop down to the ground and proceed to roll around, just like they taught us in school many years ago. Who knew I'd need to know how to do that?

My last thought before darkness descends is that I'm grateful I got the kids out. It doesn't matter about me; they're safe and so is Champ.

Matt

"We've got three new contracts," I advise when Reese calls on me for a report. "Plus, a possible fourth, but I told them I needed to bring it to the table first because it's huge."

"What is it?" Porter asks. I grin at him because as his enforcer, we've gotten close.

"Some developer wants to build a new strip mall outside of town. If we do it, we're going to need to hire another crew so that we don't keep anyone else waiting."

"We can do that," Reese advises. I see Chrome, our secretary, jotting everything down. A lot of our guys are quiet, but they're a good fit for the club. "Chrome, go ahead and get an ad worked up so we can hire on some new guys. We need people with experience, but I won't overlook anyone who is just starting out since there's something they can probably do."

I nod. "I agree. There's definitely work that the unexperienced or less experienced people can do and who knows, if they do well enough, we may keep them on because that might generate even more business."

"Gotta keep our women happy," Nick states. "And with all the babies that'll be popping out, kids as well." The room fills with laughter at his words, because the three old ladies who are pregnant are already keeping their men on their proverbial toes.

"True," Reese says. "Okay, if everyone is in favor concerning this new contract, then Matt, you reach out to the developer and let him know so we can see his plans. Now, I need to see what y'all think about expanding the tattoo parlor. We're getting busier but don't have the room to bring in another artist unless we find a bigger place."

"Why can't we build our own?" Porter asks. "That way, we make it big enough so it can expand again if we need it to."

"Man, y'all came with your 'A' games today," Reese replies. "I actually have a piece of land in mind that would be perfect, and it's already zoned for commercial use."

Doughboy, our treasurer, glances down at his tablet then over to Reese. "Is it the one off Main Street?"

"Yeah, where those old warehouses used to be. They finally razed them, so the property is ready to be rebuilt." I watch Doughboy do something on his tablet again, nodding the whole time.

"Want me to put a bid on it online?" he asks Reese.

"You can do that shit?" Reese questions.

"Yep."

"If everyone's in favor, then absolutely," Reese replies. We go around the room and when the vote is unanimous, Doughboy bends over his tablet again. When he looks up, he nods at Reese, who grins. "Kinda liking this twenty-first century electronic shit."

There's a knock at the door and I see Porter glare before he yells, "Come on in and this better be fucking good." When the prospect, Garrison, opens the door, he looks equal parts terrified and nervous.

"Uh, I'm sorry for barging in, but Matt's phone keeps ringing." As one of our prospects, he's charged with doing anything we need him to do until he gets patched in and today, he's the 'keeper of the phones' during church.

"Who on earth would be calling me? Mandie knows we have church, so it wouldn't be her, and my appointment for one potential job isn't until later."

Garrison stammers before he says, "Um, actually, that's who has been calling."

My heart starts pounding in my chest as he hands it to me when it starts ringing again. At Reese's nod, I hit the accept button then put it on speaker because I have a feeling that I'm going to need my brothers. "Mandie? Everything okay, sweetheart?"

"Is this Mandie Matchum's husband?" a female voice asks.

"Actually, her last name is Ferguson now, but yes, this is her husband. Where's my wife? Who is this?" I question, already standing.

"Your wife and children were brought into the emergency department," the voice says. "We need consent for treatment."

My mind is whirling; when I left, she was planning to stay at home because Aria had a rough night. What could've happened that all of them are at the hospital and they need consent? "Yes, go ahead, I'm on my way." I disconnect the call without even asking what happened; my goal is to get to my family as quickly as possible.

As I slip my phone in my pocket, I notice my brothers standing and they follow me out as I practically run to my bike. Without concern for our normal formation, I've got my bike started and am careening out of the club-house parking lot. It's not long before my brothers are surrounding me. While it doesn't take long to get to the hospital, I still feel as if time has stopped. We quickly park and I run to the emergency room door, grateful it automatically opens. I notice the desk and rush over there, my brothers at my back.

"Can I help you?" the nurse sitting there asks.

Before I can say anything, I feel Reese's hand on my shoulder as he states, "We're here about his wife, Mandie Ferguson. We understand she and the kids were brought in."

The nurse does something on the computer, and I see the expression on her face before she quickly masks it. "Ah, yes. Can you follow me please?" She stands and with no other recourse, we follow her into a room that's off to the side. "The doctor will be in shortly," she says before leaving.

"What the fuck could've happened? Even if Aria got worse, Mandie would've been able to give consent," I murmur.

Nick, who was looking down at his phone, says, "Matt, it looks like there was a house fire."

My heart drops and I feel like I can't breathe. Memories and flashbacks bombard me, and I find myself slipping out of the chair and onto the floor, my hands behind my neck. "Fuck. No! No, that can't be possible."

Reese, Nick and Porter surround me. "Let's just wait to see what the doctor says, brother. She might not have been able to give consent because of smoke or something," Reese says. My mind, though, is trapped in memories from a decade ago, when I was burned so badly, I thought I would die. I wouldn't wish that on my worst enemy and knowing that my woman and kids might be experiencing that has my heart breaking in a million pieces.

Before I can say anything, a doctor walks into the room. "Mr. Ferguson?" he questions, looking at all of us. Reese reaches down and helps me up, and as I walk toward the doctor, my brothers surround me. Their presence is calming, despite my terror at what I'm about to hear.

"That's me. How is my wife? My kids? What happened?" I fire off question after question, not allowing him to answer. He waits me out, however, a fact I'm grateful for because I know I'm not being rational.

"There was apparently a fire at your home this morning. Your wife got the kids out of the house but was injured in the process. We're treating both children for smoke inhalation, especially given your daughter's history."

"Where are they?" Reese asks. I'm too choked up right now and can't speak after the doctor tells us what happened.

"The children are up on the pediatric floor. We have them in the same room since they're siblings. Your wife is in the burn unit," he states. I'm torn; I want, no I *need* to see Mandie, but I know her first concern will be for the kids, so I probably should check on them first. Even though I should probably ask him what degree burns she sustained and how her body was affected, right now all I really care about is that she's alive and our kids are okay. The rest we can worry about later since she's mine regardless of how badly she's hurt.

"Let's go, brother, so you can see your kids before your wife. You know she's gonna wanna know how they are," Nick states.

I nod before saying, "Thank you, doctor. For everything." Based on how folks normally react when they see a biker in his cut, I've been very impressed that he treated us normally, instead of like second-class citizens.

"Your wife is a brave woman from what I understand. The paramedics who brought them all in said that the house was fully engulfed when they arrived. Apparently, a neighbor saw it and called it in, but didn't realize anyone was at home. It wasn't until the paramedics arrived with the fire department that they found your kids in their car seats and your wife on the ground, unconscious and injured."

Once again, my heart clenches hearing his words. I know the pain that Mandie will experience. While a lot of the nerve endings die after a significant burn, not all of them do, especially at the outer edges of the burn itself and the treatment itself is excruciating. At least I can help her through that part. As a group, we walk out of the room and toward the elevators. Reese presses the button for the pediatric floor once we're finally all inside and we wait, the tension palpable, until the elevator doors open on to the pediatric wing.

I see a nurse and ask, "Can you tell me where the two kids who were in the fire are? They're my children."

"Aria and Beau? I'm taking care of them today," she replies. "Follow me, please." We follow behind her, eliciting stares from the personnel as well as other parents, yet I don't give that first fuck. I need to put my eyes on those two babies who have wormed their way into my heart already. As we walk into their room, I can't fight the smile despite the seriousness of the situation.

Both of them are in the same bed and Aria is curled around Beau, her arm across him in a hug. I quickly pull out my phone and snap a few pictures so I can show Mandie. "They're asleep?" I question, moving so I'm at their bedside.

"We have them under sedation so that the oxygen we're giving them will help clear out their lungs," the nurse replies. "They'll likely sleep all night and I have your number on file if anything comes up. I'm sure you want to go check on your wife."

"I do, thank you." The relief I feel seeing the two of them sleeping is all-encompassing and my eyes grow wet thinking about what could've happened.

"They're good, brother," Reese murmurs. "Let's go check on Mandie."

"I'm glad y'all are here," I reply. "The only thing I don't know is where Champ is at. No one has mentioned him."

Nick looks at me then says, "I'll go see what I can find out, brother. You just take care of your family right now." I give him a chin lift before I lean over and reach through the holes in the oxygen tent so I can touch each child. Once I've put my hand on each of them and can feel their little bodies moving with each breath, my heart eases slightly.

Now it's time to go find and see my wife.

CHAPTER 14

Mandie

As I slowly open my eyes, my first thoughts are for the kids. "Aria? Beau?" I call out. I know I'm in the hospital thanks to the unrelenting beeping noises, but other than that, I'm absolutely clueless as to what happened once I got the kids out of the house. I shift in the bed and pain rockets through my left side. Spying the button to call the nurse, I press it and wait for someone to answer.

"May I help you?" the voice asks.

"Where are my children? Are they okay?"

"I'll be right in, ma'am," the voice replies.

I maneuver the bed so I'm sitting up and wait, my anxiety ramping up the longer it takes for someone to tell me what happened. When the door opens, I see a nurse come in and feel myself relaxing a little. "Where are my kids?" I question as she comes toward me.

"Let me get your vitals, ma'am," she says.

"I need to know about my kids, dammit!" I all but screech. "I don't give that first fuck about myself right now. They're the most important thing here, don't you understand?"

I see the compassion in her eyes as she starts taking my blood pressure. "They're on the pediatric floor under observation for smoke inhalation."

"So they'll be okay?" My voice is barely above a whisper. I still can't figure out how the house caught on fire. It was older, sure, but all the electrical stuff was in good shape. *Thank God for smoke detectors. And Champ.*

Champ! Oh my God, what happened to him? I voice my question out loud but the nurse shrugs. "I don't know about any dog, ma'am. And yes, your kids will be just fine. We've called your husband as well and I expect he'll be here shortly."

Matt. Dear heavens, this is going to kill him if something happened to Champ. Unable to worry about him, I decide to ask the next important question. "How badly am I hurt? I mean, I feel some pain, but mostly, I feel numb."

"You sustained third-degree burns on your upper left arm, shoulder and back. The pain you're feeling is mostly because of the treatment you've already received. We had to do what's called a debriding in order to remove the skin that's dead. But first, we had you in a saline soak in order to get your shirt and bra off because it was imbedded in your skin. You've got a pain pump next to you and it's pre-dosed, so if you need it, you can push the button. It's set up so that there's no way for you to give yourself too much."

"How long will I be here?" I ask, her words swirling in my head. *Aria and Beau are okay, that's the most important thing. So what if you're now scarred?*

"A lot of that will depend on your body, to be honest. We'll be doing the debriding treatments every day to remove the dead skin and allow the new skin to grow. As long as the wounds don't get infected, it shouldn't be more than two or three weeks," she states.

Two or three weeks? I feel the tears start streaking down my face. Other than when Aria was in the hospital, I've never been away from the kids for any length of time.

"Thank you," I murmur. I feel so defeated right now and with my pain level ramping up, I decide to push the button on my pain pump. As the medicine enters my IV, I feel my eyes grow heavy.

Matt

There's a procedure for me to see Mandie, apparently, according to the sign posted on her door. I quickly don the gown, mask and gloves, then slip on the coverings for my boots. The fact that they barely cover the top half makes me grin behind my mask. She's in a sterile environment to prevent infection, something I'm all too familiar with. "We're going to go over to the house, brother, and see if there's anything we can salvage for y'all." I nod my appreciation, my focus already on the petite woman who owns me.

I haven't told her what she's grown to mean to me. Haven't told her that I love her. Haven't let her know that if she's willing, I want more kids with her.

That changes now, I think to myself as I cross over the threshold into her room. She's asleep, the oxygen mask over her nose and mouth an indicator that she likely sustained smoke inhalation as well as burns. I grab the chair that's in the corner and carry it over to the right side of the bed, since I can see the left side is wrapped. Leaning down, I kiss her forehead, unashamed of the tears that fall from my eyes.

"Hey, pretty girl," I whisper, taking her hand in mine. I look at all the monitors and realize that she must have recently hit the pain pump. The one I had when I was injured had a red light and a green light to indicate when you could and couldn't press it, but hers has a timer that is counting down. Regardless of whether she's awake or not, I'll press it when it's time because above everything, she's going to need rest in order to heal. "The kids are okay; I just left their room. When you wake up, I've got the cutest pictures ever to show you. They're both in the same bed and Aria is curled around Beau as if she's protecting him. You did good, Mandie, so fucking good and I'm beyond proud of the fact that you got all of y'all out of the house. Nick has gone to look for Champ for me. I'm sure he's fine because he wouldn't have left your side. The rest of the brothers are at the house to see if there's anything they can salvage for us, but I've got the most important things here in this hospital — you and the kids."

She murmurs slightly but doesn't wake up, so I continue talking. "I've been remiss, sweetheart, and haven't told you exactly what you mean to me. Not only do I love you beyond mere words, but I'm in love with you. I can't imagine a day in my life without you and the kids in it. I want more kids, Mandie, with you. I can't wait to see your belly grow round as you carry the fruits of our love. I know I said things were at your pace, but this morning showed me that nothing is guaranteed, so when you get home, we're going to get started on that, okay?"

Time passes as I continue to talk to her, sharing things that no one outside of my therapist ever knew. I remind her about how Jessa's attitude toward my scars left me incapable of sustaining an erection, how I was resigned to living the rest of my life that way until she came along and I felt that urge once again. "Can't promise things won't go fast those first few times, sweetheart; hell, it's gonna be like I never did it before, I'm sure, but I'll always take care of you."

"Matt?" a voice from my past calls out. Looking up, I see Jessa now in the room.

"What the hell are you doing here?" I question. She's wearing scrubs but the Jessa I knew wouldn't be involved with burn victims, not based on how she treated me as if I were a leper. In fact, she was a paralegal then, so the fact she changed careers has me a bit perturbed. She pitched such a fit about my injuries that for her to now be in the medical field has blown my mind.

"I, uh, I'm a phlebotomist. I'm here to draw more blood to see if her oxygen levels are improving," she replies, her hands shaking.

"You're not touching my wife," I seethe out between clenched teeth.

"Your wife?" she whispers, glancing down where Mandie is lying, still asleep. I can see shock written on her face; did she honestly think I would remain single the rest of my life? I mean, I had anticipated that happening until Mandie came along, but that's for me to know, not her.

"Yes, my wife."

"Matt, I owe you an apology for how I acted," she says. When I go to say something, she holds her hand up. "Please, hear me out. When you left, I was crushed because I realized that the best thing I ever had was no longer in my life. I can't believe how cruel to you I was, and words can never express just how sorry I am for how I made you feel."

I'm stressed, frustrated, scared, which is probably why I say what I do. "Honestly, Jessa, I don't give that first flying fuck about any apology you want to make. Until I got hurt, everything was all sunshine and roses. I know that if you had been in a car accident and hurt, I wouldn't have turned my back on you. No, I would've been beyond grateful and relieved that you were still alive. You didn't give me that same fucking consideration. You called me a monster and told me I was repulsive. Do you have any fucking clue how that fucked with my head? No, you don't and quite frankly, I don't care if you ever understand what you did to me. Thankfully, I have a family in my life who doesn't give a damn if I have scars or not and this woman lying right here? She's the strongest, kindest person I've ever met. Now, find someone else to draw her blood because you'll never touch *any* part of her. Do you understand?"

Jessa flees from the room, tears flowing down her face while I try to calm myself down. I've never been more livid than I am right this moment. Does she honestly think a few pretty words will erase the emotional damage she wrought? Fuck that shit. A few minutes later, another person in scrubs comes into the room, causing me to look away from Mandie's face.

"Mr. Ferguson? I'm Cody, another phlebotomist. I'll be doing the blood draw on your wife if that's okay?" I look at the slight nurse standing there; he's only a few inches taller than Mandie, but I can tell from his actions that his first concern is the patient he's caring for as he washes his hands then puts on a pair of gloves.

"That's fine," I reply, moving back. From memory, they usually draw blood on the opposite side from any injury, so I know he'll need to be where I'm at.

"You can stay where you are if you'd like, this won't take long," he advises. I watch as he expertly sets up the tourniquet, cleans the area, then quickly inserts the needle. Within a minimal amount of time, he has two tubes drawn and is removing the tourniquet. All without Mandie so much as crying out, which I find impressive as hell.

"How long before you know anything?" I ask.

"The doctor put a rush on these tests, so as soon as I return to the lab, the technician will be working on them."

"Thank you." I go back to staring at my wife, my mind drifting to all of the what-if's that could've happened.

What if I hadn't changed the batteries last weekend? What if I had been home? Would she and the kids have gotten hurt? Guilt swamps me, even though I logically know that there's not much else I could've done differently than it appears that she did.

"I wish you'd wake up," I whisper, my hand smoothing back her hair. I know they cleaned her up, but her hair still smells smoky and I wish I could wash it for her. Since getting married and moving in with each other, I've grown accustomed to the scents that make her unique. She's the perfect old lady, too. Nothing seems to faze her, even though I know that she's still dealing with demons from her own past based on the nightmares that have woken me up most nights. I wish that fucker was still in town; I'd find a way to make him pay for ever causing her harm. However, him not being around will make it that much easier for me to adopt Aria and Beau according to our club attorney. Because his rights were terminated after he beat Mandie, the attorney said that we shouldn't have any issues and don't have to deal with the notifications that typically get published in the paper. My guess is that he's long gone, and we won't hear a peep from him.

My phone rings and I answer it when I see it's Nick. "Hey, brother. Did you find him?" I ask before he can say a word.

"Yeah, brother. The firemen took him to the vet we use and he's there being treated."

My heart sinks hearing that Champ is hurt. "What's wrong with him?"

"He's got a few burns on his paws, as well as a few places on his back from burning embers. He also suffered some smoke inhalation, but Dr. Webb says he'll be fine and not to worry. She'll take care of him until y'all get home."

"Thank God. I knew he probably didn't leave them, but it honestly didn't cross my mind that he would be hurt as well."

"He's a good dog, that's for damn sure," Nick replies.

"I owe him a fucking steak dinner from Juan for saving my family."

Nick chuckles before saying, "Yeah, I think he'd like that for sure. Reese said they didn't find much at the house, but what they got, they brought to the clubhouse and put it in your room. Well, except for the clothes; the old ladies took those and are trying to get the smoke smell out. Found two baby books as well. They're charred, and they smell like smoke of course, but they're going to air them out as well. Not much else, brother."

"The most important things survived, brother, and that's all that matters," I tell him. "If anything had happened to Mandie, the kids, or Champ that was worse than what they suffered, it would've killed me." I'm not lying there; she breathed new life into mine the day I saw her for the first time at The Steakhouse.

"Well, y'all were planning to move so while you're dealing with them at the hospital, we'll put the old ladies and the prospects on shopping and stocking duty. No doubt they won't mind handling that at all."

I chuckle because he's definitely right about that fact. Even Mandie has said she can't believe how 'do or die' the old ladies are when it comes to dividing and conquering when they shop. "I know we're all gonna need a new wardrobe from the sound of it. Old man Smithers was leaving the furniture we decided on, and the rest was going to be delivered tomorrow."

"We'll take care of it. You just worry about your family, brother. Reese said to tell you that was an order," he advises, laughing.

"Glad y'all have our backs because I honestly don't think I could leave here if I wanted to," I admit.

"We'll get you some clothes up there, brother, so you don't have to leave. Corrie also said she heard from Juan and they're donating twenty percent of the proceeds for the next two weeks to y'all to help y'all out. Oh, and Juan and Maria are going to be bringing food up to y'all as well."

"Mandie's still sleeping, Nick," I advise.

"Well, you have to eat, brother. Oh, and Shayla picked up some pajamas for the kids to wear instead of those 'stupid hospital gowns' as she calls them. She dropped them off at The Steakhouse and Maria and Olive plan to head up there shortly. Since they're family, they're going to alternate staying with the kids so you can focus on Mandie."

"Gonna need a new stuffed Poppy and Olaf," I say. Aria loves her 'babies' and those two didn't survive from what I understand.

"Believe it or not, Poppy was in the car. Olaf, however, wasn't, so I'll add that to the list. We've got you, brother. Later," he says, before disconnecting.

The emotions swarming through me at what he just imparted have me crying, something I haven't done in a long ass time. "God, Mandie, we're so fucking fortunate to have the family we do," I murmur, my hand squeezing hers. "You just need to focus on getting better because all of them are taking care of the rest of it."

CHAPTER 15

Mandie

I've been in the hospital for a week and Matt hasn't left my side, despite my assurances that I'll be okay. A slight infection at the wound on my left shoulder has me on heavy-duty IV antibiotics, which make me sick. I won't let him come with me when they take me for the burn treatment, however. I haven't even looked at them yet, afraid to see just how bad it looks. Today, the nurse handling the debriding told me that things were looking better so I feel slightly encouraged. Right now, I'm waiting on Matt to bring Aria and Beau in to see me. They were only in the hospital for two days and have been with Juan and Maria since then because Matt refuses to leave me alone.

Hearing Aria's voice, I look up and see him walking through my door, all three of them in gowns and masks.

"Mommy! Did you knows that Champ is okay? We is too, Mommy. When does you come home?" He sits them on my bed and cautions them both about being careful, even though Beau, as a baby, has no clue what he's saying. Still, I relish their weight against my right side and smile at him through tear-filled eyes.

"Thank you," I whisper. I wasn't sure how much longer I could go without seeing the two of them but had to wait until my infection cleared up.

He leans in and kisses my forehead before replying, "Anything for you, pretty girl."

I raise my left arm a bit, nodding at the protective covering that they replace every day after treatment, and state, "Not so pretty anymore."

Tilting my chin up, I have no choice but to look at him when he states, "You'll always be my pretty girl, Mandie. No amount of scars, inside or out, will ever change that, do you hear me?"

I'm about to reply when Aria pipes up and says, "I got a new Olaf, Mommy. Him burned up in the fire."

"I know, sweetie. Thanks to Champ, though, we're all safe and that's what's important, right?"

She turns her sweet face to me and says, "But you got hurt, Mommy, when you was carrying me and Beau."

"Aria, that's my job, sweetie, as your mommy. I'll always do what I can to protect you both. I'd do it again in a heartbeat even if it means I'm here getting better instead of at home with y'all." I know she doesn't really understand, but I feel like I have to say it.

"Well, some of my favorite people are in the same room," Juan says, walking in, gowned and masked, with several bags of food.

"Juan," I protest. "Y'all have done so much for us."

"Haven't we had this discussion before? You're family," he replies, before he proceeds to set up a delicious lunch for us all. "Did you give Matt the information to call your insurance agent?" he asks. "And do we know what caused the fire?"

"The fire chief called and said that apparently, there was some built up lint in the dryer. The screen itself was clean, but hell, I had no clue that it could get inside and build up, so I'm pretty sure that Mandie wouldn't have known either. About the insurance agent, I called them the other day for her," Matt states. "They're going to want a statement for their file, but I've forwarded all the pictures to them. Your landlord uses the same insurance company as you do so he's going to get information from that adjuster. I'm glad you had it, sweetheart."

I nod because even though sometimes it was a pinch, at least I had coverage on the contents. I wish I had known that lint could do that, though, and make a mental note to talk to Matt about how we can prevent something like that from ever happening again. Thankfully, the SUV was far enough away that it didn't sustain damage. I had argued with Matt when he bought it for me, saying I didn't need a new vehicle, but he told me that I was carrying precious cargo and even though my car was now roadworthy, he'd feel better if I was in something that wouldn't break down. He also argued that he didn't fit very well in my car, which was definitely true. The cool thing is, he found a teenager who needed a car and we gave him a great deal.

"We can use it when we need to buy stuff for the new house to replace what was lost," I say, only to see both Juan and Matt give each other a look. "Okay, what was that about?" I try and fail to give them my 'mom look' which has both of them chuckling at me.

"Well, you see, once word got around to some of the clubs we're friendly with that we had a house fire, they decided to do a poker run and give us the proceeds," Matt cautiously announces.

"Plus, when folks found out that their favorite waitress was in the hospital, they've been extremely generous," Juan adds.

"What exactly does that mean, Juan?" I question.

"I let it be known that twenty percent of the daily profits would be going to y'all," he advises. "And before you say I can't, I most certainly can do that for my family. But the customers weren't satisfied with just that and they started leaving money with notes saying that it was for you and your family."

My tears overflow at the sheer generosity of this small town I live in. It doesn't matter how much or how little comes in, it's the thought that they cared enough to part with their hard-earned money that makes me cry. That and the fact that ally clubs are doing a run for us? Yeah, I break down completely. For so long, I've pinched and scrimped, doing without for myself to make sure that the kids were taken care of and from the sound of it, those days are long gone. Of course, they already were, seeing as I'll be working as the club bookkeeper, plus waitressing for a little while longer. "This is mind-blowing to me," I admit. "I mean, my insurance policy was pretty good. It would definitely cover the contents." I don't mention the sentimental items I lost. I'm heartbroken that I don't have the kids' baby books any longer. At least Beau's didn't have much in it, but Aria's was full to the brim.

"We can always take it and start college funds for the kids," Matt says, wiping my tears away. "Well, for whatever they want to do that is because they may want to learn a trade instead."

"I like that idea a lot," I murmur. An idea pops into my head and I decide to share it. "Matt? I know that all the pictures I had of the kids are probably gone, but all the ones I took of them I saved to the cloud. I'm pretty sure my laptop didn't survive either, but do you think we could get another one and reprint them?"

"I'll go pick up a laptop for you today," Juan asserts.

"Juan, who is minding the restaurant right now?" I question. He's so hands-on that I'm surprised that he's brought food for us every single day.

"Maria, of course. She's probably harder on the staff than I am," he says, winking at me. I can't help myself; I giggle. The two of them have definitive rules for their employees, but they treat all of us as an extension of their family and it's a fantastic environment to work in.

"I can't wait to get out of here and resume a normal life," I say. I mean, I enjoy spending so much time with Matt. We've spent hours talking in between visitors, and what he's shared has made me fall deeper in love with him. I haven't told him just yet. I figure I'll wait until we actually leave the hospital.

"Soon, sweetheart. The important thing is, you're getting better," Matt states.

"God, I sound so whiny and I don't mean to, I swear! I have loved all this time with you, Matt, but what about your business? What's happening with all of that?"

"My brothers have stepped up, Mandie. Not only that, but I've got a good crew in place already. You don't need to worry about that at all, okay? My place is right here, beside you," he emphatically announces.

"Eat, eat, before it gets cold," Juan instructs. "Then I will take the little ones to Maria and get her out of my kitchen."

Giggling, I help Aria with her food while Matt takes Beau and starts feeding him. The normalcy of the situation, despite the environment, makes me smile even bigger. I never thought this is what I'd want, yet here I am, married to a man who has quickly become my best friend. He's held me while I cried in pain and soothed my worries countless times.

"I love you." He freezes when the words pop out of my mouth. When he looks at me, his eyebrow raised, I can see the hope in his eyes. "I mean it, Matt. I love you." Once again, I realize how unconventional we are with regard to our relationship. Hell, we haven't even had sex yet, for Heaven's sake!

He hands Beau over to Juan, then picks Aria up and gives her to him as well. Cupping my face in his large hands, he leans in until our foreheads are touching and whispers, "I love you too, Mandie. So fucking much it hurts when you're not near me. I was never more scared than when I got the call from the hospital and seeing you, so tiny, lying in the bed obviously injured, broke my heart in a million pieces. Please don't scare me like that again."

"I'll do my best, honey," I murmur. He gently kisses me, and I feel the promise behind his action. I have no clue what life holds, but I know as long as he's by my side, I'll be able to handle it.

"That's my cue to head on out," Juan says. "You two lovebirds need some time alone."

Matt

After Juan leaves with the kids, I maneuver myself into the bed next to Mandie and pull her into my arms. "I'm not sure this is allowed," she whispers, as if she's afraid a nurse will fly into the room.

"Sweetheart, where do you think I've been sleeping all these nights?" I ask.

The look she gives me has me chuckling because I usually wait until she's asleep before I hold her all night long, then wake up before she does. The nurses have all seen me holding her close and not one of them has said a damn word to me. Not that I give a fuck; she's my wife and if me holding her keeps the nightmares at bay, then that's what I'm going to do.

"Really?" she asks. Her body and eyes show that she's in pain, so I press the button since she's been stubborn lately. "Matt, I don't want to sleep again," she protests.

"You need it to heal, pretty girl," I reply, kissing her nose. "And it's my job as your husband to make sure that you rest."

I grin when she rolls her eyes at me. "Whatever," she replies, yawning.

"Take a nap, sweetheart. I'll be here when you wake up."

CHAPTER 16

Mandie

I'VE BEEN HOME FOR A WEEK NOW AND STILL haven't looked at my injuries. I go daily up to the outpatient center for them to clean and re-dress the wounds, and then I do physical therapy. Surprisingly, or at least to me, anyhow, Matt's brothers and the old ladies moved us into our new house. I was blown away when Matt drove us up to the house and I saw it. They even painted the kids' bedrooms and got them set up the way I imagined a kid's room should look. Aria is in a princess phase and they managed to find a bed that looks like a carriage. Granted, her room looks as though someone vomited pink and purple everywhere, but it's adorable. They strung fairy lights around the ceiling and painted the walls to look like she was in a castle out in the woods. There are tiny animals peeking from around trees and they even have trolls everywhere. It's a wild combination but somehow, it works.

Beau's room is a tiny biker's dream. They found someone who crafted an awesome bed for him as well, mindful of the fact that he's still a baby. The rails on the sides can be removed once he's old enough, but right now, my boy sleeps in a motorcycle. It's the coolest thing I've ever seen and whoever made it definitely did a great job. The headlight even serves as a nightlight! The rest of his room has various biker insignia everywhere and there's a 'road' painted along his wall that makes it look as though he's riding.

They even set up our new office. Matt and I have matching desks that are far enough apart that we still have our own space. I've got a desktop as well as a laptop and all the information I need for the businesses has already been downloaded. Corrie plans to come over later this week to help me get stuff started.

"Mandie? Where are you at, sweetheart?" I hear Matt, but don't reply. I'm standing in our bathroom facing the mirror. It's time for me to see the damage. I'll never regret my actions because losing my babies wasn't an option. I'm just worried about how Matt will react. I mean, it's not like I was perfect before anyhow, but the scars from the burns are a little more 'in your face' than the silvery stretch marks across my hips and lower abdomen. I figured today was as good a day as any since Ollie has the kids overnight. Tomorrow, we're doing a combination birthday party for Aria, as well as a house-warming get-together.

With my eyes closed, I slip my shirt off my body, then the camisole, which is the only thing that is soft enough right now. "Here it goes," I whisper to myself before I open my eyes. I know from where the nurses scrubbed each day where I got burned but seeing it is a different story. "Oh my God," I cry out, looking at the skin that's stretched and marred across my upper arm and shoulder. Turning slightly, I can see where my clothes burned into my skin. As the tears fall and my vision gets blurry, I don't hear the bathroom door open, nor the man who I love with everything I have walk up behind me.

Gentle kisses touch the mangled skin as he strokes his hands down my arms. I continue to cry despite his ministrations, unable to stop the wave of emotion crashing through me. He turns me and pulls me into his arms and holds me as the past few weeks run down my face and I sob into his shirt. "Shhh, I've got you, pretty girl, you're okay," he murmurs.

"I don't know what I expected," I stammer out. "I don't regret it, but honestly, Matt, what can I do to keep the kids from being afraid of me?"

He picks me up and carries me into our room and sits me on the end of the bed. "You know we've talked about how I was hurt on my last mission, right?" he asks me. I nod, watching his face. "Keep in mind that most of my scars are now covered with tattoos, but they're still there."

"Did Reese do them?" I ask.

"He didn't start them, another artist did, but he's done all of my work since then. He has the skills and if you want, once everything is fully healed up, you can get tattoos as well. But I'm telling you right now, I don't give a flying fuck if you do or don't because they show me, you're a survivor. You're still here, the kids are still here. Hell, Champ is still here. Because of you, Mandie. Just like I'm still here because of Jackal." His voice breaks and I see his eyes start to glisten as he slowly pulls his shirt off then turns.

On his back I see a 3D tattoo that looks so lifelike, I have to touch it. Standing, I move closer and only then can I see the damaged skin underneath the beautiful artwork that spans his back and runs down his left side. The dragon is so lifelike I half expect it to breathe fire or something. Seeing the scars has my tears flowing once again. I know the pain he endured, and it was far worse than what I dealt with, that's for sure. Starting at the top, I kiss along each scar, my tears dripping onto the colorful skin. I can see it goes further down and nudge him a bit. "Let me see the rest, please," I murmur, my own scars temporarily forgotten.

I see him take a shuddering breath before he undoes his jeans and lets them fall, then he slips his boxer briefs off. The dragon continues across his left ass cheek then wraps around to the front. I kiss each scar, blushing a little at the proximity, before I move to the front. "It's not pretty," he warns.

"Oh, honey, the pain you went through," I cry, looking at the beauty that was wrought from the agony he suffered. The tail of the dragon goes down his thigh and I see that despite the seriousness of what he's showing me, his erection is proudly jutting out. I gulp a bit, wondering just how in the hell it'll ever fit inside me, but my eyes are on the dragon. The head comes over his left shoulder and the dragon's arm circles underneath his arm to rest at the center of his chest where a treasure box sits. I can see he's had new work done and start crying harder when I realize that in each of the baubles that are in the chest, he has one of our names with mine being over his heart. There's even room for more, should we have kids down the road. "It's beautiful," I finally say, looking up at him. "I can't believe you did this." My fingers trace each of our names, along with the date we got married.

"You and the kids are my treasure, sweetheart," he replies. "Are you sure the scars don't bother you? You don't find them repulsive?" I can hear the uncertainty in his tone, and it breaks my heart knowing that another woman put those doubts in his head.

Deciding to take the biker by the dick, I move closer to him and reach down to caress him. "Not one bit, honey. You're still the most handsome man I've ever known and right now, all I gotta say is her loss is my gain. Please, make me yours, Matt. I think we've waited long enough, don't you?"

Matt

Her words break the final chain that I didn't know was wrapped around my soul. She doesn't care repeats in my head as I draw her close and kiss her with every ounce of passion I feel. When she sighs, I invade her mouth with my tongue and soon, our tongues are dueling with one another. It's not like I haven't kissed her before, but it's different this time. It's a claiming kiss. One filled with hope for the future and a promise that together, we can overcome anything life throws our way. I pull back slightly, breathless, then pick her up and carry her to our bed.

Once we're laying side by side, I caress her face and say, "I love you so fucking much I don't know that there are words that can express what I'm feeling."

"I feel the same way," she admits.

"I honestly don't know how long I'll be able to last when I finally get inside you, sweetheart, so I want to explore a bit."

"I uh, I've got stretch marks," she says, her voice low.

"From carrying two children, pretty girl. Does it feel like they turn me off?" I ask, grabbing her hand and guiding it to my dick, which is harder than it's ever been.

Her soft giggle makes me smile as she slowly strokes me. Too much of that and I'll be coming in her hand, not in a pussy that I know will fit me like a glove. I lean in and capture her lips with mine once again. Kissing her is quickly becoming my favorite thing in the world to do.

She leans in closer and I feel her nipples graze my chest. Moaning softly, I reach up and start stroking her breasts. Soon, her moans mingle with mine and I can feel her desire as she presses against me. I move and begin peppering her jaw and neckline with kisses, causing her to writhe, so I toss a leg over hers. "God, Matt, it's never been like this before."

I can feel the sense of urgency swirling around us both but at the same time, despite her words, she's not pressing for more than I'm giving her. Leaning down, I capture one of the raspberry colored nipples in my mouth and begin nipping and sucking on it while my hand plumps the other breast. "You smell good enough to eat," I mumble, causing her to giggle.

When I look up at her, she shrugs and says, "That tickles, honey." I smirk as I switch sides, giving the other breast the same attention, while my hand strokes down to her hip. Cupping her ass, I draw her closer and groan when I feel the heat emanating from her pussy. As my hand moves toward the apex of her thighs, I can feel her desire leaking from her core. Swiping my fingers through, I bring them to my mouth and suck them in while she watches, her face flushed.

"I knew you'd taste good," I murmur as I move down her body until I'm situated between her thighs. "Open for me, sweetheart," I command when she closes her legs tight.

"No one's ever done that," she whispers. I can see she's nervous, but at some point, she'll realize that I want nothing between us whatsoever. I want it all – the good, the bad, the ugly. So I do what any self-respecting biker would, I lean in and swipe my tongue through her folds anyway. The moan that erupts from her mouth has me grinning because with little effort, I soon have her legs over my shoulders and my mouth planted against her pussy.

"Based on how addictive your taste is to me, you'd better get used to it," I advise before I start eating her pussy like a starving man. When I insert a finger, she moans, and I feel her pussy clench. "Do you like that, sweetheart?" I murmur.

"God, yes," she stammers. "Please don't stop, Matt." As I continue in my mission to make her shatter, I add a second finger then search for her G-spot. Once I've found it, I apply pressure as I suck on her clit. Her back arches up and a keening cry escapes her as her pussy practically breaks my fingers when her orgasm hits. I don't stop, wanting her well-lubricated for me since I'm not a small man in stature or dick.

"Give me another one, pretty girl," I command.

"I-I can't," she says.

"Yes, you can," I advise, thrusting my fingers in and out as I lap at her pussy. When I feel the unmistakable flutters again, I double my efforts until she's screaming my name, then I continue until all that's left are occasional shudders. Crawling back up her body, I line my dick up at her entrance and slowly, almost reverently, start pushing inside.

Despite two orgasms, she's still tight and my eyes cross at the sensation. I continue, using shallow thrusts until I'm fully seated, my groin pressed against hers. "Matt," she whispers, her eyes bright and her face flushed.

"You doing okay?" I ask. At her nod, I begin making love to her. Despite the fact that it's been a long fucking time since I was in this position and I really want to pound into her until she's screaming, this first time is special.

In.

Out.

Swivel.

In.

Out.

Swivel.

I can feel the sweat forming on my forehead and watch as it drips onto her chest which is heaving in excitement and passion. "I love you," she pants out, her hands circling my shoulders.

"I love you too," I reply. "So fucking much. I need you to come, Mandie, because I don't know how much longer I can hold on."

One of her hands snakes between us to where we're joined but instead of rubbing her clit, she splays her fingers around us, adding another sensation that has me closer to coming. "I'm close," she whispers, her hips thrusting upward on my downward thrusts.

I feel my balls tightening when her pussy begins fluttering. Once again, she clamps down, only this time it's on my dick and the utter perfection of this moment has me calling out her name as I fill her with my cum.

I continue to rock gently as the aftershocks course through both of our bodies, leaning in and kissing her gently. Instead of withdrawing, I roll so that we're still connected but she's on top so I can run my hands down her back. "That was fucking phenomenal," I advise, kissing her.

"Never in my life did I think it could be like this," she replies.

"It's only going to get better, the longer we're together," I state.

CHAPTER 17

Mandie

I WAKE UP DELICIOUSLY SORE THE NEXT MORNING with a smile on my face. Feeling the heat against my back, I realize that he truly doesn't care about my scars and that realization is so freeing, I feel tears well up. "What has you awake so early?" his sleepy voice questions. I turn so we're face-to-face and kiss his jaw.

"I love you," I whisper. "And it dawned on me that this," I say, pointing to my arm, "doesn't bother you in the least."

"Why should it? It's a part of you, sweetheart. It also shows that you survived something horrific," he replies. "And for the record, I love you too. But we need to get up and moving so we can get ready for everyone."

I shriek when he hauls me out of the bed, tosses me over his shoulder and proceeds to head into the bathroom.

"Matt, I have to pee," I hiss out. He sets my feet on the floor and smacks my ass as he points me in the direction of the little 'room' that houses the toilet. I actually like that aspect of our master bathroom. There are some things I'm just not comfortable doing in front of him and using the toilet is one of them. I don't care what we did the night before, some things are just private.

I hear the water go on in the shower while I'm doing my business and once I'm done and have flushed, I come out and proceed to wash my hands. "You know we're getting ready to take a shower," he advises, watching me.

"It's a habit, honey," I reply, drying my hands. He proceeds to pull me into the shower and show me what all the fuss is about where shower sex is concerned, then washes me thoroughly.

I've spent the morning making side dishes to go along with the meats that Matt is currently marinating. The smells have my mouth watering and I realize that we didn't eat breakfast. I proceed to whip up a couple of sandwiches for us and head out to the back deck to give him one. When I see that several of the prospects are currently decorating for Aria's birthday, I let out a little gasp.

"She's going to be so excited," I state as I see a kid-sized bouncy house being erected. It's got multiple layers, for lack of a better word. There's a slide side that goes into a shallow pool filled with water, and off to the other side, a castle.

"Figured she would like it," Matt says, coming up behind me and wrapping his arms around my waist. He nuzzles my neck before dropping a kiss behind my ear. The sheer intimacy of his actions has me melting into his body and I feel him move with his chuckles.

"I'd better get back to it," I reply even though I'd rather do nothing more than to stay in his arms. He lightly smacks me on the ass, and I head back inside. I know Maria is making Aria's cake and Juan plans to bring food as well. I don't think it'll go to waste, however, seeing as the whole club plans to be there, as do Juan, Maria and Olive.

"Love you, sweetheart," he says, pulling me back for a kiss. Despite how many times we connected the night before, I immediately want him again and moan. "There'll be time for that later, pretty girl," he murmurs against my lips.

"I sure hope so," I sass. I'm not sure where this newfound attitude is coming from, but I suspect it has everything to do with the man whose arms are wrapped around me.

Matt

As I supervise the prospects getting everything set up for the party, I think about how drastically my life has changed ever since I met Mandie. I went from a man who planned to live a solitary existence, save for my club and my brothers to standing here, in our home, with a wife and two kids. Champ comes up alongside me and leans against my legs. I reach down and scratch behind his ears. The fur that burned is starting to grow back and his paws are finally healed. "So glad you were there that day," I state. As if he understands, he looks up at me, tongue lolling out to the side, and wags his tail. "Yeah, you love them too, don't you?" I can't wait until Beau is old enough to toddle after Champ and I suspect that 'my' dog will be watching over him much as he does me. He's actually the reason we figured out that Aria was having a bad night.

Since we got married and moved in together, he is constantly making his rounds. He's still there for me when a nightmare hits, only now, he checks on the kids. That night, I had gone back to sleep after another harrowing dream about my team, when I felt his nose against my neck. I got up and he led me to the kids' room where I found that sweet girl wheezing in her sleep. Mandie, hearing the noise, got up behind us and within minutes, had Aria hooked up to her nebulizer. Then, she spent the rest of the night getting up and checking on her, which is why she was lying down the morning of the fire.

"Need anything else done, Matt?" Garrison asks.

I look around the yard and see the coolers sitting out. "Let's go ahead and get those filled with ice. Break them down to kid drinks, sodas, and beer. I'll go make some signs we can put on the tops, that way folks know what they're getting."

"Got it," he replies before heading out the back door. I grin when I see the huge play area that my crew helped me build. We even built a mini playhouse that looks like our house for Aria. They haven't seen it yet, so I grab the huge bow to wrap it up.

Once I'm done, I head back into the house to see Mandie putting stuff in the fridge. "Let me help you with that," I say, walking over and taking the huge bowl out of her hands. My task accomplished, I turn around and pull her into my arms and proceed to kiss her senseless. "God, I love you so fucking much," I murmur once I pull back.

"I love you too," she replies. "Are we ready for the invasion?"

I chuckle because she's been a whirlwind, making sure the house is spotless, cooking and baking. "Sweetheart, I think it's perfect. Come outside and let's relax before we're invaded."

Several hours later, our house and yard are full of people. I'm still laughing at Corrie, Shayla and Kirsten. All three are in the throes of their pregnancy cravings and seeing my brothers walking in, their arms straining with bags of their old ladies' preferred snacks which the women promptly descended on and are now ensconced in chairs under a shade tent, stuffing their faces, started the hilarity. "Don't laugh, brother, Mandie will probably do the same thing once you knock her up," Reese warns, watching his old lady.

"Can't wait, if I'm being honest," I reply, my eyes on the kids who are swinging and sliding. Aria and Meli are currently holding court in the bounce house and Beau is crawling around in the sandbox, making car noises.

"Yeah, nothing like them, that's for sure," Nick states. He's made multiple trips out to Shayla and I swear, if he could, he'd wrap her up in cotton and not let her lift so much as a finger.

"Looks like y'all have settled in pretty well," Reese observes.

"Thanks to y'all, brother," I say. "By the time she came out of the hospital, y'all and your old ladies had pretty much taken care of everything for us. Appreciate it more than I can say."

"Y'all are family and that's what we do," Juan says, coming up to where we're huddled by the grill. It's not just any grill either; it's one of the biggest I've ever seen, with multiple cooking surfaces as well as what looks like burners that are on the side for those dishes that use pans. Right now, every surface is cooking something; we've got steaks, ribs, chicken, hot dogs, hamburgers, and brats. I'm not sure what my woman was thinking but looking at the number of people in our yard, I don't think we'll have a lot of leftovers.

"Glad y'all could make it, Juan," I tell him.

"We wouldn't miss this for the world," he replies. "I knew the day she walked into The Steakhouse, Aria on her hip, that she was going to be a part of my family, y'know?"

"I can believe it. She's one of the strongest women I know and that's saying a lot because I think the other old ladies are as well."

"We've done well, brother," Porter states, slapping me on the back and handing out beers.

"Yeah, we have. We're all blessed fuckers," I say.

"Not sure we should use that word in conjunction with being blessed, but it works, so fuck it," Nick retorts, causing all of us to laugh.

"Maria has the cake inside, so it doesn't melt. We also brought ice cream," Juan advises.

Reese starts laughing harder, doubling over and slapping his knee. "We- we brought ice cream too," he wheezes out. "Corrie has been craving it, so she made me stop at the store. I think I picked up five gallons. It's out in the freezer in your garage, brother."

"Fucking hell," I mutter. "You're taking what's left back home, Reese."

Meanwhile, Nick is slumped against the outside of the house, holding his ribs and laughing like a fucking lunatic. "What the fuck, brother?" I inquire.

"You've got sausage biscuits in there as well," he stammers. "Shayla's on a kick with them and eats two or three at a time, even in the middle of the night." I see a look on his face and think that he's enjoying those late-night snacks of a different variety and grin.

"Sounds like the hormones have gone nuts," I observe.

"No complaints, though," Reese states, smirking.

Rex, who is once again manning the grill, yells, "The meat's done!"

The old ladies immediately get up and start making their way to the overladen tables to make plates for the kids. I head inside and grab the high chair for Beau, then take the plate that Mandie was making for him and finish the job. "I got this, pretty girl," I tell her, kissing the top of her head. She grins at me and nods.

Once we're all seated, Reese stands back up and says, "Matt, Mandie, need y'all to come up here for a minute." I take her by the hand and stand next to my club brother and president, my arms now wrapped around her. He grins at me and I give him a chin lift.

"Okay, so y'all know that a poker run was done by some of our allied clubs because of the house fire. I got that check yesterday and Porter and I decided that the club was going to match what was made. Here's a check for fifty thousand, y'all." Mandie looks up at me and I can see her eyes glistening. Hell, I'm trying to hold my own emotions back right now, so I hug her a little tighter and kiss her ear. "That's not all, though. Juan here gave this to me yesterday as well. As y'all may or may not know, he donated twenty percent of the profits from The Steakhouse for two weeks. Not only that, but Mandie's regular customers gave him money as well. Here's another check for thirty thousand dollars, plus this envelope stuffed with cash. No clue how much is in there, but it's full, that's for sure."

"I can't believe this," she whispers. "I'm blown away by everyone's generosity." So am I if I'm being truthful. We just got the insurance check two days ago for the contents of her house.

"Reese, don't forget the other stuff," Corrie calls out, standing and holding a bag.

"Thought I'd let you handle that, slugger," he replies. She smiles at him and walks toward my woman, holding out the bag.

"The guys found these when they were going through the house. They're a little bit charred, but we managed to get the smoke smell out." She reaches into the bag and pulls out the two baby books and I watch as my woman loses it, dropping to the ground and clutching the books in her arms.

"I thought these were gone," she whispers, her hands rubbing across both books. "Beau's didn't have much in it yet, but Aria's definitely did, and it broke my heart that those little memories were gone."

"There's more, Mandie," Corrie advises, pulling out another book. It's a photo album and I realize immediately what the old ladies did for my wife. She had given me the information for the pictures that were on the cloud and when I was asked, I passed it along, not thinking anything more about it. They printed off all the pictures and put them into a huge photo album, which Mandie is now flipping through, her hands stroking the tiny faces as they appear on each page.

When she finally looks up, tears streaking down her face, she says, "Nothing, and I mean nothing, not the money donated, not the insurance check, not this envelope stuffed with cash means more to me than these three things right here. Aside from the fact that my babies and dog are safe, the only things I secretly cried about were the pictures and the kids' baby books and y'all fixed even that. I swear y'all are superheroes in leather cuts or something."

Her comments have everyone laughing, and I take that opportunity to help her up, wrapping my arms around her. As I lean in, she whispers, "I'm beyond blown away, if there is such a thing, Matt. I can't believe they did this all for us."

"We're a club, a family, sweetheart, and my brothers and their women will go balls to the wall for each and every one of us," I reply.

"Can I has cake now?" Aria asks, breaking the emotional scene. While us adults were busy listening to what Reese had to say, then watching as Mandie saw the baby books then the photo album, my little princess was busy eating.

"Let us grownups finish eating, sweetie, then we'll do cake," Mandie promises.

The rest of the day is spent with my family, laughing and enjoying one another. By the time the kids went to bed, they were just about asleep already. After checking the house and making sure all the doors and windows are locked, I head into our room to find Mandie curled up on the couch that's in our sitting area. Her smile has my heart accelerating as I move closer and sit next to her. "So, where were we?" I ask as I pull her into my arms. She's freshly showered, and I breathe in her scent.

"I think my husband was going to have his way with me," she teases, running her hand across my chest until it lays across my heart.

"Guess he better get on with that then, huh?" I reply, taking her lips with mine.

CHAPTER 18

Mandie
Six Months Later

"Harder, Matt," I plead, as he thrusts into me from behind. His eyes are glued on the tattoo that rests on my left hip proclaiming me as his. The injured area is still not ready to be tattooed, but Reese has already drawn something that I fell in love with and the minute the doctor gives me the okay, I plan to get it done.

"Your pussy is like a glove, pretty girl," he pants out. Ever since that first time, we can't keep our hands off each other and I have some news for him today that I think will blow his mind. He reaches underneath me and when his fingers strum my clit, I detonate, my pussy clenching on his dick so hard I fear for its safety.

"Matt," I keen out, thrusting back as I fly higher.

He yells out my name as he stills, and I feel his cum shooting deep inside. Spent, I collapse onto the bed and will my breath to calm down. I feel him kiss the biggest scar on my shoulder before he rolls onto his side and pulls me into him. "Gets better every fucking time," he growls out. I love his voice, but especially after we've had sex. It's all raspy and growly and shoots tingles throughout my body.

"I honestly never knew it could be like this," I admit. Alistair was obviously a selfish lover, only I had no clue since he was my first and only before Matt. Hell, I read a lot and never realized that some of the other positions I read about in my books were real; I just thought they were fiction. Matt has changed all of that, however. It's as if he's making up for lost time and I'm definitely not going to complain.

He growls again and says, "Don't like to think of anyone else inside what's mine, pretty girl."

I grin into his chest; he's possessive without being over-bearing, that's for damn sure. "So, what's the news you had for me?" he questions.

"How do you feel about becoming a family of five?" I reply, looking up at him. I watch the myriad of emotions cross his face before he breaks out in a smile so breath-taking that I gasp.

"You're having my baby?" he asks, his voice low as his hand strokes down my side to cup my still-flat stomach.

"Yeah, in about seven months or so," I state, my hand covering his. "Looks like more kids for the Black Tuxedos are on the way." Corrie and Shayla both had their babies, little girls, and I've watched two burly bikers turn into mush. Of course, I've heard the mumbled comments about maybe opening up a gun store, so they're prepared for the time when 'little assholes with dicks' start sniffing around.

"How soon will we know the gender?" he questions, his hand rubbing my stomach, as if he's trying to feel the baby. I honestly can't wait until he can because the sensation is unlike anything I've ever felt. I know it'll be different from his perspective, of course, but Alistair wasn't really involved when I was pregnant with Aria, and I was alone during Beau's.

"My next appointment, hopefully," I reply. "I hope you'll be able to come."

"Wild horses couldn't keep me away, sweetheart," he asserts.

"You know one good thing about being pregnant?" I ask.

"No, what's that?"

"I'm really horny all the damn time," I whisper, nuzzling his neck.

"Is that so?" he inquires, his hand moving to my hip.

"Mmm-hmm," I mumble, already feeling my desire ramping back up despite the fact that we just finished not too long ago. I can't get enough of him and spend my time during the day when he's gone thinking of us together. Doesn't matter if I'm doing the club's books or cleaning the house, him and his talented self is at the top of my list, all day, every day.

"Well, it's a good thing I'm up for the challenge," he replies, rolling me until I'm flat on my back with him hovering over me. As he kisses me, I feel him thrust inside, our earlier combined release making it easy.

Soon, the only sound in the room is slapping flesh and our moans. As my orgasm nears, I cry out his name and the emotions that crash over me have tears coming to my eyes.

"You okay, pretty girl?" he asks once we've caught our breath again.

"Must be the hormones because I've never been better," I state, wiping my face. "We've made a mess." I start giggling because I just put clean sheets on the bed earlier in the day and now, they need to be changed again.

"How about you go get a bath started and I'll change the bed," he states, helping me up. "I'll be in shortly." I grin as I make my way to our bathroom to do as he suggested. I love 'bath time' with my man. I always get dirtier before he makes sure we're both squeaky clean.

Matt

As I remake the bed with clean sheets, I grin. I had suspected, based on her recent behavior, that she was probably pregnant. She's not much of a crier, per se, but lately, even commercials have her weeping. The biggest thing, though, is her breasts are bigger. Now that it's confirmed, I think the grin on my face will be permanently etched there. Never in my wildest dreams did I suspect while lying in that hospital bed overseas, so fucking broken and damaged, that I would be where I am right now. Married, with two kids, and another on the way. "Thank you, Jackal," I murmur as I carry the used bedding to the laundry room. I get the washing machine set up but don't start it just yet since she's filling the tub. "If you hadn't pulled me to safety, none of this would've been possible."

Walking back through the house, I check on each kid. Aria is almost unfindable amidst all of her 'babies', but I finally locate her, straighten her out and make sure she's covered before I kiss her gently on the forehead. When I reach Beau's room, I stifle a laugh. He's upside down with his legs dangling over the side. Once again, I go about making sure he's more comfortable before kissing his forehead. Now that he's turned one and walking, he's busy all the time so when he falls asleep, he's out until morning. I hear the soft thump of Champ who is next to Beau's bed. Leaning over, I scratch between his ears and state, "Keep a watch out, buddy, okay?" His tail wags faster as if he's agreeing. "You're a good boy, Champ." A soft woof is his reply before he lays his head down on his paws again, his eyes on the little boy in the bed.

Once again in our room, I strip down and walk into the bathroom. It's time to bathe my wife. I grin when my dick hardens; guess he's on board with my plans as well.

EPILOGUE

Seven Months Later
Matt

WE'VE BEEN IN CHURCH FOR THE PAST HOUR, GOING over all the businesses and getting an update on everything. "We're all in agreement about the new business then?" Reese asks us. We decided to open up a gun and ammo store, partly because of the little girls that Reese and Nick had, and partly because there wasn't a shop like we wanted that was closer than two hours away. We've got a gun range as well and are setting up gun safety classes.

"Absofuckinglutely," Nick replies. "Gotta make sure my girl is protected." Laughter rings around the room at his comment as Reese nods. "No pencil-dicked fuckers will get near her," he continues. "Not on my watch, anyway."

"How's Kirsten?" I ask Porter during a lull. She had a rough pregnancy and ended up on bedrest for the last three months, but she finally had the baby, a little boy, about a month ago.

"She's good now that he is sleeping most of the night. I swear, I thought I was married to a zombie," he grumbles. "Not that I'd ever tell her this, but she was looking downright scary up until the past two weeks. Same clothes, hair a disaster, crying all the time. I'm glad you suggested she see her doctor, Reese, because it seems she had a slight case of post-partum depression. They've gotten her started on some medicine and already, I can tell a difference."

"How's Mandie?" Reese questions.

"According to her, she's as big as a hippo and she doesn't understand how that's possible seeing as she barely gained any weight with the other two," I reply. "I told her it probably had more to do with her actually being able to eat this time around than the size of the baby and that did not go over very well."

"Slept on the couch, huh?" Nick jokes.

"For three fucking days," I retort. Until I forced my way back into our room and our bed, that is, but they don't need to know that part.

"When she has the baby and has healed, we can get started on her tattoo," Reese advises. "Her skin is more than ready now." I nod; the only reason she had to wait is because she got pregnant. Of course, we weren't exactly trying to prevent that so I can't complain.

"Alright, back to business," Porter states. "It seems like our reputation is getting out there because I got contacted by a huge corporation that wants us to put a bid in for their new corporate headquarters they plan to build on the outskirts of town. It would bring a bunch of jobs to the area, which is a plus, but I'm not sure if we can handle something that large or not."

"We can do it," I affirm. "Got a great crew plus there are others who we can add to help. Can you email me the information so I can work up a bid?" He nods at me and I make a mental note to take a ride out to the job site.

Reese is about to say something when there's a knock at the door. My heartbeat starts to accelerate as I remember the last time it happened when we were in church. Porter's snarl has the door slowly opening and I see the prospect, Garrison, standing there, my phone in his hand. "Uh, Mandie's calling, Matt."

I reach for the phone as it rings again, giving me a sense of déjà vu. "Hello?" I ask when the phone connects.

"My water broke while I was at the sanctuary. Corrie is taking me to the hospital. Please tell me you're heading that way as well?" she asks without taking a breath. I hear her breathing like they taught us in that class we attended and grin.

"On my way, pretty girl. Where are the kids?"

"Shayla has them. We were showing the kids the new puppies that were born when it happened, so she has all of the kids except Kirsten's because she wasn't with us."

"I'll let Nick know, sweetheart. I'm on my way now. Don't have the baby until I get there."

Her huff of laughter makes me chuckle as she states, "Um, if I start having to push, I will whether you're there or not, so you'd best get the lead out, mister."

"Love you, Mandie. I'm leaving now," I advise, standing and pulling out my keys. I notice that my brothers are doing the same and grin, knowing that they'll have my back like always.

"Gotta go, I need to focus, honey. Love you too." The call disconnects and I look at my brothers.

"We're having a baby today. Gotta go."

Reese smirks before he hits the table with his gavel and says, "Church dismissed. Let's go welcome the newest Black Tuxedos MC member in style, y'all."

Mandie

Corrie drove us to the hospital like hell hounds were chasing us, but right now, I'm glad for her expediency, since I'm fully dilated, and the baby's head is crowning. "Where is he?" I grunt out through a contraction. "He promised he'd be here."

"They just pulled up," Corrie says, looking down at her phone. "You're doing great, by the way."

"It's the third one so hopefully, I learned something with the other two." I don't mention that I was all alone in the birthing room except for the nurse and doctor when I had Beau. Maria and Olive were watching Aria at the time.

I feel the need to push and am silently crying inside that Matt might not make it when the door bursts open, and he walks into the room. The gown he's wearing is too small, so it's torn and ripped, and the mask is pulled below his chin. "I'm here, sweetheart. You doing okay?" he asks as he rounds the bed and takes my hand.

The contraction hits before I can respond, and I squeeze his hand until I feel his fingers roll together. Once it passes, I look up at him and say, "I'm sorry, honey."

"Okay, Mrs. Ferguson, you're ready to really push now so on the next contraction, I want you pushing while your husband counts to ten, okay?" I nod at her, too focused on breathing to verbally answer. She looks at the monitor next to her and despite the fact that she knows I can feel the contraction, she says, "Here we go."

Long moments pass as I push for everything I have, Matt's strong body behind me as he supports me while counting. When I flop back, the doctor says, "Again, Mandie, the baby is almost out." Once more, I push, my only focus on getting the watermelon I've been carrying out of my body. I hear a soft cry as the doctor states, "Congratulations, Mom and Dad, you have a beautiful baby girl."

I'm sure I'm the only one who hears Matt's whispered, "Fuck me," but I can't help it, I start giggling.

"You okay, honey?" I ask when I see his dazed look as he gazes at our daughter who is now lying on my stomach.

"Just thinking that it's good that the gun store was approved," he replies, reaching out a finger and lightly stroking it down her cheek. "She's beautiful."

"She's covered in yuck, Matt," I state, even as my hands come up and cradle her tiny butt in them. "And I don't give the first fuck."

His laughter rings out and I grin up at him. I know I'm probably a hot mess right now, but he makes me feel beautiful, wanted, and cherished no matter how I look.

"I love you, Mandie Abigail Ferguson," he whispers as he leans in to kiss me.

"I love you, too, Matthew Allen Ferguson," I reply. "Now, what should we name our little girl?"

The End

Author's Note

For those of you who read "Hale's Song", you probably noticed that Reese and Corrie's son, JJ, met Hale and Addy's son, JD, as well as their nephew, Johnny. Some time in 2021, two more books will be added to the Black Tuxedos MC that will encompass the stories of JJ, JD, Johnny, Meli, and Rosie!

Stalk Darlene here

Website:
www.darlenetallmanauthor.com

Facebook Author Page:
https://www.facebook.com/darlenetallmanauthor/

Darlene's Dolls Group Page:
https://www.facebook.com/groups/
1024089434417791/

The Insiders:
https://www.facebook.com/groups/
280929722515781/

Newsletter Subscriber Link:
http://eepurl.com/dEaxGj

Amazon Author Page:

https://www.amazon.com/Darlene-Tallman/e/
B01LC3YKAY/

Goodreads:
https://www.goodreads.com/author/show/15709175.
Darlene_Tallman

Bookbub:
https://www.bookbub.com/authors/darlene-tallman

Also by Darlene Tallman

The Black Tuxedos MC My Book

1. The Black Tuxedos MC - Reese My Book

2. Nick - The Black Tuxedos MC My Book

Bountiful Harvest My Book

His Firefly My Book

His Christmas Pixie My Book

Her Kinsman-Redeemer My Book

Operation Valentine My Book

His Forever My Book

Forgiveness My Book

Christmas With Dixie My Book

Our Last First Kiss My Book

Draegon: The Falder Clan - Book One My Book

Scars of the Soul My Book

Hale's Song My Book

Paxton: A Rogue Enforcers Novel My Book

Mountain Ink:Mountain Mermaids Sapphire Lake My Book

Poseidon's Warriors MC

Poseidon's Lady My Book

The Mischief Kitties (with Cherry Shephard)

The Mischief Kitties in Bampires & Ghosts & New Friends,
Oh My! My Book

The Mischief Kitties in the Great Glitter Caper My Book

The Mischief Kitties in You Can't Takes Our Chicken
My Book

Rebel Guardians MC (with Liberty Parker)

Braxton https://books2read.com/u/bzax09

Hatchet https://books2read.com/u/bpWerJ

Chief https://books2read.com/u/3L97EJ

Smokey & Bandit https://books2read.com/u/47ZMvg

Law https://books2read.com/u/b0ZWx1

Capone https://books2read.com/u/49Dkdw

A Twisted Kind Of Love https://books2read.com/u/4AJYaA

Rebel Guardians Next Generation (with Liberty Parker)

1. Talon & Claree https://books2read.com/u/bO6ZJo

2. Jaxson & Ralynn https://books2read.com/u/b5re27

3. Maxum & Lily https://books2read.com/u/3RareG

New Beginnings (with Liberty Parker)

1. Reclaiming Maysen https://books2read.com/u/mgLaXX

2. Reviving Luca https://books2read.com/u/bowjn9

3. Restoring Tig https://books2read.com/u/mqvQMd

Nelson Brothers (with Liberty Parker)

1. Seeking Our Revenge https://books2read.com/u/m2vnxO

2. Seeking Our Forever https://books2read.com/u/m0rkaW

3. Seeking Our Destiny https://books2read.com/u/4Ekk6l

Old Ladies Club (with Kayce Kyle, Erin Osborne and Liberty Parker)

1. Old Ladies Club - Wild Kings MC https://books2read.com/u/mVr7Br

2. The Old Ladies Club - Soul Shifterz MC My Book

3. Old Ladies Club - Rebel Guardians MC My Book

4. Old Ladies Club - Rage Ryders MC My Book

With Various Other Authors

Poetry: Dreams You Catch My Book

Made in the USA
Middletown, DE
15 April 2023